THE VAMPIRE IMPRESARIO | BOOK I

THE TENOR'S SHADOW

J.B. WARRICK

The Tenor's Shadow is a 50,000-word MM vampire romance with a guaranteed HEA and no cliffhanger. It contains a strong-but-silent vampire bodyguard and the high-strung opera singer that falls fast for him. It also contains explicit, open-door romance and the violence you might expect from a vampire story. Not suitable for readers under 18.

Content Warnings for *The Tenor's Shadow*

Blood
Grief
Violence
Imprisonment
Character injury and death
Strong language
Sexual content
Explicit sex

1

ANTHONY

"**I cannot sing with this belt cutting off my circulation!**"

Anthony was being ridiculous, but he didn't care. He'd already talked to the general manager of the Chicago City Opera twice about the costume designer, and she'd continued to put him in clothing that made him look like a string of variably sized sausages.

Every time he looked in the mirror in his dressing room, he cringed. Yes, he was short and high-waisted, and yes, his ass was perhaps larger and juicier than the average tenor, but he knew he could look better than *this*.

Maestra Svoboda cut off the orchestra and rolled her eyes behind her wire-framed glasses. Anthony didn't care. Let them all wait. If the CCO wanted a world-class performance, it needed to provide a world-class costume design. There was no way he'd be out there singing high C's looking like a lumpy eclair.

The patrons shifted in their seats. Guilt stirred in Anthony's chest, but he quickly shoved it away. The audience had known what they were getting into coming to an invited dress rehearsal.

Dress rehearsals were paused for technical issues all the time, and this issue was both technical and very personal. The seats were probably filled with aging opera queens, anyway. He hated to look petty in front of the public, but they'd eat the drama up.

When something wasn't right, it wasn't right.

"Antonio, my apologies." The general manager of the opera was a thin little man in his sixties. Well, maybe little wasn't fair. He was the same height as

Anthony, just under five-foot-seven. But where Anthony had a solid Italian build with thick thighs, the GM was skinny, almost frail-looking.

His name was Barry, of all things, and his daily uniform matched the tenor of his name: an oversized and wrinkled button-down shirt hanging down over a pair of khakis that pooled slightly at his feet. He wore a close-mouthed smile — a thinly veiled attempt to fake compassion and understanding — but he wouldn't be winning an Oscar anytime soon.

"It's too late for sorry, *caro*," Anthony said. "I've had several meetings with you about what's-her-name—"

"—Michelle."

"Yes, Michelle. A painfully ordinary name for a painfully ordinary woman. You and I have spoken about her multiple times, and yet here we are at final dress, and my costumes still look like they're from a community theater production of *Saving Private Ryan*. I'm supposed to be a dashing prince!"

Don Ramiro, the lead tenor in Rossini's *La Cenerentola*, was one of Anthony's favorite roles. He got to be handsome, a skosh devious, occasionally mean, and he sang *"Si, ritrovarla io giuro,"* one of Rossini's most impressive arias.

"Antonio, I promise we'll take care of it, but we need to continue—"

Anthony reached down, unbuckled his belt, ripped it off, and threw it into the wings. Was he throwing a temper tantrum? Maybe, but it was justified. He was tired of his concerns being ignored, and he refused to look foolish onstage. He'd long left behind the "suck it up and take it' portion of his career.

Besides, it's not like making a scene would hurt his reputation. A little fiery repartee just enhanced his diva image.

Anthony locked eyes with Barry, who was slowly backing away. "Where is she now?"

"Who?"

"Michelle, the costume designer, where is she?"

"I'm right here!" The normally soft-spoken woman burst from the stage wings, her voice ringing like a trumpet playing a loud, flat note. Her long gray hair was pulled tight in a ponytail, and her beige peasant skirt flowed around her as she strode across the set.

"I have been designing productions here for twenty years, and I have never worked with such a spoiled brat!"

Normally, she exuded a sturdy, calm Midwestern charm. Anthony liked angry Michelle better. He preferred an adversary with some fight in them.

"You'd think that someone with that much experience could make a pair of pants that could fit around my ass." Anthony smirked at her. This was going to be a blast.

She came to a stop a few feet away from him, her hands tucked into her bulky gray designer's apron.

"All the most famous sopranos love my costumes. I shouldn't have to worry about the opinions of a pipsqueak tenor whose sense of fashion includes crop tops and booty shorts."

"Those are my rehearsal clothes! At least I don't go out in public dressed like I'm planning on churning butter at the commune." Anthony pursed his lips in excitement. It had been a while since he'd had a decent argument.

"Please, let's calm down..." Barry was sweating. Good.

Michelle ignored the general manager. "Perhaps you don't enjoy my designs because they make you seem like a human man, instead of the lizard person you actually are."

"Shouldn't you be off somewhere weaving hemp knapsacks?"

"You...you...your high notes aren't even that good!"

Unable to help himself, Anthony burst out laughing.

"Now we both know that's not true," he said. "If you think that, your hearing must be as off as your sense of taste."

Michelle's face turned beet red. She shrieked in frustration and hurried back to the wings.

Before exiting, she spun around and locked eyes with Barry, who was frozen in terror. Anthony could feel him vibrating from ten feet away.

"Are you going to let this flash-in-the-pan insult me like this?" Her tone was deadly.

Barry stared at her. "I..."

As he trailed off, she threw up her hands. "Asshole," she grunted under her breath as she disappeared backstage.

Barry turned back to Anthony, deep exhaustion showing in the lines of his face.

"Antonio..."

"Here's what's going to happen." Anthony took the tone he used when he knew he had the upper hand, and disagreement was not an option. "My assistant can give you names of some local costume designers that will have no problem working around the clock to polish this turd into something tolerable."

"I won't fire Michelle."

"I'm not asking you to fire her. I'm telling you

that a different designer is making my costumes."

"Antonio…"

"Otherwise, you might find that I've come down with bronchitis on opening night."

Barry's eyes went wide. His mouth opened, but no sound came out. That was the signal for Anthony to wrap this up. The audience was getting restless, and he'd played with his toys for long enough.

"Jennifer!"

Anthony's personal assistant appeared instantly, as if by magic. A tall woman in her mid-twenties, she had a demeanor more like a wealthy heiress than a PA. She threaded through the chorus of men milling about the stage, her high heels clicking against the boards as she made her way to Anthony.

"What?" She didn't even make eye contact, instead typing furiously away at her phone, commenting on a picture of a bulldog puppy in a cat costume.

Anthony shook his head, smiling. He'd never been able to get her to act professionally, but she was too good at her job for it to matter. He hoped she was working on his social media accounts and not hers, at the very least.

Who was he kidding? He loved how blasé she was. It was endlessly entertaining, especially when people underestimated her.

"Take Barry here up to his office and give him the info for our Chicago costume designers." Anthony gave the still-speechless man a once-over. "Stop at my dressing room on the way and pour him a glass of whiskey."

"Fine."

Jennifer headed off at a clip, with Barry trailing helplessly behind her. As they disappeared into the darkness of the wings, Anthony turned to the company, plastering on his most charming smile.

This was what he excelled at. Was he temperamental? Sure. But he also knew how to keep people happy. He could get away with the occasional tantrum if everyone felt special.

"My friends, I'm so sorry for the disturbance. I know this dress rehearsal didn't go the way you'd expect. You are all consummate artists, and it's an honor to create this new production with all of you." It wasn't a lie. Anthony had seen how hard they'd worked. "If you'll indulge me, please join me at the bar tonight. Drinks are on me."

A murmur ran through the company. The reaction was mostly positive, which didn't surprise him. He was an expert at damage control. It wouldn't be a cheap night, but it was worth it to not have to wear what's-her-face's hideous costumes.

He turned to the pit. "Maestra?"

The conductor's face exuded a frustrated world-weariness, mostly directed at him. Anthony didn't mind. He'd gotten what he'd wanted. The conductor picked up her baton, and the orchestra launched into the cabaletta of "Si, ritrovarla."

"Dolce speranza, freddo timore, dentro al mio core stanno a pugnar."

Anthony's voice rang out from the stage, bright and present, echoing back to him all the way from the last row. The audience members' faces shifted from looks of confusion to surprised enjoyment. That was the thing about Anthony. He knew he could be frustrating, he knew he could be demanding, but when push came to shove, he was worth the trouble.

Anthony's clear tenor filled the theater. His sound always bloomed once things went his way. Now that he had dispensed with the awful costumes, he could give himself fully to the character and the music. His heart swelled as he built to the triumphant high note, his soul pouring out through the clarion metal of his voice.

The bar that Jennifer had chosen was perfect, no surprise there. It had an old school Italian vibe, with dark wood and antique light fixtures that cast an amber glow over the room. It made Anthony think of his nonna's favorite restaurant back in East Hanover, of Friday nights eating chicken parmigiana.

"Oh my god, your high notes sounded so good tonight. You *ate.*" The cute twink chorister touched Anthony on the chest.

Probably in his late twenties, the guy didn't have many years of twinkdom left, although he was holding on tight to his youth with his dyed blonde hair and his tank top and parachute pants combo. They were in direct contrast with Anthony's dark hair and classic suit.

Evidently, the twink had gotten enough liquid courage to make his move.

"Thank you, *tesoro.*" Anthony winked at him. "You looked great in your army uniform. Very butch."

The chorister blushed a bright pink. "I was worried the pants made me look like a twig."

"Not at all. You can't hide that perfect ass of yours."

The chorister pressed in closer to Anthony,

purring and earthy like a furtive viola. "I don't want to hide it. I want to show it off."

Anthony leaned in to whisper in his ear, catching the scent of sour apple shampoo wafting off his hair. "I'd watch that show."

A voluptuous figure approached them, wrapped in scarves and dripping with stylish, over-the-top jewelry. She was practically gliding as she made her way across the crowded bar. Her red lipstick appeared burgundy in the dim lighting. Anthony kissed the twink on the cheek and squeezed a handful of his perky ass. The blonde man giggled, sighing and tracing a pattern on Anthony's stomach with his fingertips.

"You can put on your show later tonight in my hotel room," Anthony said. "Go chat with the others. I'll grab you on my way out."

The chorister smiled and stepped back. When he saw who was coming, he nodded and scurried away.

"You'll break his heart, you know." Her voice was low and mellifluous, the rich, dark sound associated with Eastern European singers.

"Lena, I'm surprised you came out." The Polish mezzo-soprano usually retreated to her hotel room after rehearsal. "A bar doesn't seem like your scene."

"I'm not drinking, darling." Lena kissed Anthony on each cheek before raising her glass of clear liquid and giving it a shake. "Club soda. I'm surprised you are, though."

"It's two whole days until opening. Plenty of time to recover." Anthony downed the rest of his whiskey and set the glass on the bar.

"Drunk and flirting with some chorus boy. You must leave behind a string of broken hearts in every city."

"Oh please." Lena was being so awkwardly straight, one of Anthony's least favorite things. Why did the heterosexuals make such a big deal about sex? "Everyone knows that I'm leaving in two weeks. No surprises."

"I've seen that boy looking at you during rehearsals. It's pure infatuation. He's going to sleep with you because he thinks that's all he can get from you."

"He's not wrong." Anthony shrugged. It was the nature of the thing. He didn't have time for relationships. His schedule was grueling, and anything more than a one-night stand was baggage he couldn't afford.

"People aren't secondary characters in the story of your life, *Anthony*."

"Don't call me that." Anthony looked around, anxiety spiking in his chest. Hopefully, everyone was too tipsy and involved in their own conversations to overhear.

"You may pretend to be Antonio Bianchi, heartthrob Italian tenor, but I knew you when you were Tony Bianchi, commuting to grad school from his grandma's house in New Jersey."

"Only my nonna calls me Tony." Lena was really getting on his nerves. He appreciated her honesty, but he liked his illusions. Being Antonio made him feel larger-than-life and brave, not like scared seven-year-old Tony, who lost his parents in a car accident.

"Fair enough, dear." Lena took a sip of her drink, her lips leaving behind traces of burgundy on the glass. "But people aren't disposable. You can't toy with their hearts. And you can't throw fits every time someone puts you in an outfit you don't like."

"The pants were cutting off my breath!"

"Were they?" Lena raised an eyebrow. "Because to me, it seemed like you stopped a dress rehearsal and tried to get a costume designer fired because you thought she made you look fat."

"That's not—"

"Doesn't matter. The people around you have feelings."

"They're all happy now!" Anthony gestured to the packed bar. It was filled with laughing, tipsy singers and musicians. "They're having a great time!"

"Except Michelle, I'd imagine."

"She's bad at her job. She doesn't get to be happy." Anthony was speaking louder now. He was tired of being provoked. "I don't understand why you're being so awful."

"*I'm* being awful?" Lena drained her glass and put it on the counter. "Darling, I've been your friend for a long time. Even the most talented of assholes eventually get fired. You won't always be able to get out of it by batting your eyelashes and buying everyone drinks."

"I..." Anthony was stunned. The whole point of having friends was for them to be nice to you. Tough love was for other people.

"Now, I need to get my beauty sleep." Lena kissed him again on both cheeks and drifted away through the chattering sea of tipsy musicians. As she reached the door to the bar, she turned and called out a last goodbye.

"Have fun with the chorus twink!"

2

ANTHONY

n the elevator, Anthony kept his hand planted on the chorus twink's ass. It was the perfect balance of squishy and firm, and he had plans for it. The smell of lemon-scented cleaner filled the metal box as they ascended to the twenty-first floor. The chorister, just tipsy enough to really loosen his tongue, was going on about his own career.

"I know that it doesn't happen very often, but

people do move from the chorus to principal roles. I tried to get Barry to hire me as your cover, but he said I wasn't ready for it. Said my coloratura wasn't up to snuff. My coloratura is excellent, thank you! He said that he'd consider letting me cover Don Ottavio in *Don Giovanni* next season, which would be amazing. But not as cool as if I'd been able to cover *you.*"

The elevator dinged, and the doors opened onto Anthony's floor.

"We're here." Anthony grabbed the chorister's hand and pulled, hoping the jolt would shock him enough to stop talking about his operatic ambitions. Anthony doubted he was principal role material, and even if he was, didn't he understand it would put them in competition?

"Oh my god, everything's so nice."

The chorister looked around at the hotel hallway, which, in Anthony's opinion, was only okay, a fairly ordinary attempt at an elevated mid-century modern design. The guy's eyes traveled down to the carpet, where he became entranced by the geometric pattern. Anthony pulled again. The chorister would focus once he had Anthony's dick in his mouth.

Anthony waved his key card in front of the lock, flipping the light to green. He pushed the door open and brought the twink inside.

"Holy shit." The chorister stopped in his tracks, his eyes like saucers. "This place is amazing."

It should be. Anthony had fought for it in his contract. It was the hotel's penthouse suite, and it had a full kitchen. Not that he cooked when he was on the road, but it was nice to have the option. One entire side of the suite was a gorgeous view of the lake. To the far right, the gleaming lights of the Chicago coastline jutted out into the waters of Lake Michigan. Views like that were one reason that Anthony loved to sing in different cities.

But this was no time to admire the skyline. Anthony had other things to admire.

He wrapped his arms around the taut, toned body of the blonde twink, embracing him from behind. Anthony's hands traveled up under his shirt and grazed the soft skin of his torso. The twink leaned back against Anthony's body as Anthony kissed his collarbone, making his way up his neck. When Anthony nibbled at his ear, he moaned, soft and deep.

Anthony's cock began to harden, and the twink pushed his perfectly round ass back against Anthony's crotch. Feeling Anthony's rigidity through his pants, he groaned, rubbing up and down against it.

Anthony sucked harder at the chorister's neck, who shivered uncontrollably at the assault.

"Oh god...yes..."

Anthony loved this, loved when his partner lost control at his touch. He always put himself in the driver's seat in these kinds of interactions. Technically, he was versatile, but he couldn't imagine bottoming for some stranger he met on the road. It required a vulnerability that he wasn't willing to give.

It wasn't just about topping and bottoming. He relished the power to make someone fall apart in his hands. Sometimes he imagined letting someone else have that control over him. He wondered if he would feel a sense of freedom, finally giving over everything to another person. Not that it mattered. It couldn't happen. He didn't trust anyone that much.

"Sir?"

The word snapped Anthony into the present moment. The blonde knelt on the floor in front of him, his once-innocent face filled with lust. His hands were on Anthony's waistband.

"Can I?" the twink asked.

Anthony reached down and ran his hand through the man's floppy blonde hair. He moved back a few steps until he was leaning against the kitchen island. "Go ahead."

The twink scooched forward, squeezing Anthony's erection through his pants before tugging at his belt buckle. He was so eager, so willing to please. His soft hands pulled the length of Anthony's cock out into the cold hotel air. Anthony relaxed his head back, letting it fall to the side.

That's when he saw it.

A single, large white peony lay against the black granite, and next to it, a piece of expensive cardstock covered in ornate silver calligraphy.

"Shit." Anthony reached down and removed the twink's hands from his dick. "Stand up."

"What?" The chorister had a sad, hurt look on his face, like a kicked puppy. "What did I do wrong?"

"Nothing, nothing," Anthony answered, waving him off. The twink stood awkwardly as Anthony leaned over the paper. He knew what it would say.

Dear Anthony Lorenzo Bianchi...

The chorister's arms wrapped around his waist from behind, and Anthony tensed. He grabbed the twink's wrists and pried off the body of his would-be lover.

"Listen, uh..." Shit. Anthony couldn't remember his name.

"Connor!" the chorister replied, his voice cracking with indignation.

"You need to go, Connor."

"But, I thought..." Connor's bottom lip trembled.

"Me too, kid, but I'm just not feeling it." Anthony pulled out his phone and sent a quick text. "My car service can send someone over to bring you home."

"Oh. Okay." Anthony didn't have time to take care of Connor's feelings. He had to handle the problem in front of him. Besides, Connor would be jumping into bed with some new tenor-of-the-week soon enough.

"Sorry, *caro*."

Connor turned, walking towards the door with painfully slow steps, as if he expected Anthony to change his mind. When his hand touched the doorknob, he looked back. Anthony crossed his arms.

"Tell the driver where you want to go. It's on me."

Connor shook his head and left. Too bad. They might have had fun. Oh well. He turned back to deal with the offending letter.

Dear Anthony Lorenzo Bianchi,

This is your final warning. If your uncle doesn't give us what we want, we will deliver the next message in person, and you won't like what comes with it. Tell him we wait for what is owed us.

> *Regards,*
>
> *The Azarian Coven*

These people were insane. This was the third letter in a month. One in Vienna, one in Houston, and now here in Chicago. If he was home in New York, he'd be worried, but they had only left the messages in hotels. He assumed his stalker had been bribing the cleaning crews.

It was beautiful handwriting, Anthony had to give them that, but that didn't make the letters less concerning. He hated to get the police involved, but what were his other options? Hire a private investigator?

It didn't make any sense. What did his Uncle Daniel have to do with anything? Maybe the stalker read an article where Anthony had talked about their relationship, about how Daniel had raised Anthony after his parents died, and they assumed they could extort money out of him.

If they wanted money, why didn't they ask him for it directly? His uncle was recently married. His new husband seemed well-off, but if you were going to break into the hotel of a rising opera star to leave an extortion letter, why wouldn't you go for the biggest fish?

Damn. He'd have to call London.

Anthony sat in the too-cushy armchair and took out his cell phone. It had been a few months since he'd spoken to his uncle. He hadn't meant to ignore his uncle's messages. His schedule had been packed. He loved Uncle Danny! He'd just been busy, that's all, and sometimes faraway family didn't feel as important as the opera he was currently performing.

Daniel picked up on the first ring.

"Anthony! It's about time!"

Anthony smiled at the excitement in his voice. Daniel somehow even made guilting him sound loving. He was sweet and kind. Anthony was sure it had been a big adjustment, but Daniel had been the perfect person to take in a grieving seven-year-old. He'd never let Anthony feel like a burden.

"Hey Uncle Daniel." Anthony hung his head sheepishly, even though there was no one there to see it. "Sorry I didn't call sooner."

"No problem, sweetie." Anthony heard the sound of a mug being set on a countertop. Daniel must be having one of his daily five cups of coffee. "It's three a.m. in Chicago! What are you doing up?"

"How did you know I was in Chicago?"

"Oh, sweetie, I always keep track of your schedule. You never know when Oliver and I might show up for an opening night."

"Don't surprise me, Uncle Daniel. You know I can get you tickets." They'd had this conversation before, and despite Anthony's best efforts, it always went the same way.

"We can afford them. Use your free tickets for your friends."

"I have plenty of comps." Anthony shook his head in frustration. Daniel never let Anthony take care of anything. "But that's not why I called."

"Do you need money, honey?"

"No. I'm doing very well. I promise."

"Sure, but things change, and you know, capitalism. I know how health insurance is as an artist, one broken bone and you're thousands of dollars in debt."

"I don't need money. Please don't worry about me breaking a bone."

"Well, I know you break a leg every night!"

Anthony heard a deep chuckle in the background. "Is that Oliver laughing at your terrible dad joke?"

"When I tell it, it's an uncle joke."

Anthony smiled. He really did miss his uncle. Daniel was his only family, and it had been too long since they'd seen each other.

He'd have to book more gigs in London. He couldn't take time off to visit. At least, he wasn't willing to take time off. Every empty week in his calendar was a week closer to being forgotten by audiences and by the companies that hired him.

"Is something wrong, hon?"

Anthony wasn't sure how he'd managed to let himself get sidetracked. It was just nicer catching up with his uncle than thinking about his stalker problem.

"Listen, Uncle Daniel, something a little strange has happened. Someone left a letter in my hotel room."

"A letter?"

"Written in silver ink. It's happened a couple of times before."

Anthony rubbed his eyes. Finding the letter had short-circuited his lust and tamped down his buzz. Now he was just tired. He read the contents out loud, dreading his uncle's response.

"This was the third letter?" A deep, masculine voice rumbled from the phone. It didn't belong to Daniel.

"Oliver, is that you?"

"Answer me. This is the third time this has happened?"

Anthony prickled at the demand. He didn't enjoy being ordered around. Oliver wasn't even a blood relation. Hell, he and Daniel had only been married a couple of years.

"Yes. The third in as many cities. The first time I thought it was a prank. The second, well...I was just too tired to take it seriously. Three seems like...but it's not that big a deal. Opera has its fanatics. It's some old queen with a record player and a lot of free time—"

"And it's signed by the Azarian Coven?" Oliver's sharp tone cut through the long distance between London and Chicago. "All of them have been?"

"Sounds like some kind of homegrown cult, right? Guy's probably a fundie or something."

"You need to come here," Oliver said. Anthony bristled at the command.

"What are you talking about?"

"You need to come to London. We can keep you safe here."

Anthony's forehead tensed up. What the hell was Oliver talking about?

"I don't see how you could keep me any safer there than I am here. And the next few months are nuts. First San Francisco, after that Barcelona, and then I'm making my debut in Naples. I can't disrupt my schedule."

"I'm not giving you a—"

Daniel cut off his husband, saying something that Anthony couldn't hear. He closed his eyes and willed his shoulders to relax. He shouldn't have called in the first place. If the letters hadn't mentioned his uncle, he wouldn't have. They deserved to know, but he wasn't letting them stop him from living his life.

"Anthony, honey?" It was Daniel again.

"Uncle Daniel, I'm not sure what's gotten into Oliver, but—"

"Sweetie, I know that you can't come here. But you *are* in some danger. Oliver's sending a bodyguard."

"What are you talking about?" This was always the problem with Uncle Daniel, and evidently with Oliver. With the slightest sign of trouble, they turned into huge control freaks.

"I can't have a bodyguard," Anthony continued. "They'd just get in my way."

"Let us help you."

"Absolutely not. I'll go to the police, file a restraining order or something."

The blare of loud argument burst through the phone receiver. Anthony couldn't make out any of it. He breathed in and out slowly, calming his nervous system. How could someone he loved as much as his uncle make him so crazy?

"No police, Anthony."

Anxiety stirred in Anthony's gut. Why shouldn't he get the police involved? Something was weird here. Well, even weirder than the stalking was to begin with.

"What is this all about?" Anthony needed to get to the bottom of this.

"Listen, Oliver sometimes deals with some shady businessmen, and one in particular has turned out to be, uh...deep in the mob. Things have gone south. The guy must have seen one of your articles. He's...not great."

"Azarian? Is it the *Armenian* mob?"

"...yes?"

None of it added up. Why was Daniel being so evasive?

"This is insane. Nothing is going to happen to me. I'll go down to the station and—"

"No police, Tony!"

This was serious. Uncle Daniel never used Anthony's childhood nickname.

"Why not?"

"They're...they're involved."

Daniel was hiding something important. Anthony was sure of it. Something worse than shady business dealings.

"So the UK cops are in bed with the mob.

Shouldn't make any difference in the states."

"No cops."

"Then I'll hire a PI—"

"No."

Anthony sighed, kneading his brow with his fingers. "I shouldn't have called you."

"Honey, I really—"

"No bodyguard, Uncle Daniel."

"But—"

"No. I'll deal with it on my end. I'm going to bed, I have to rest up for opening. Please tell Oliver that I'll be perfectly safe. Love you."

Anthony hung up without waiting for an answer. Stubbornness ran in the family, and he and his uncle were evenly matched in that department. If he didn't quash the whole bodyguard thing, he'd wake up tomorrow with an entire security team outside his door.

He stripped down, leaving his clothes in a pile on the floor. The hotel dry cleaners could deal with it tomorrow. He got under the covers and willed sleep to come, ignoring the unease fluttering in his stomach.

Tomorrow, he would sleep late, rest his voice, and forget all about the stupid letter.

3

FREDDIE

Freddie was stalking his prey in King's Cross when he felt his master's Call. He'd watched silently from an adjacent rooftop as a rogue vampire drifted through Granary Square, looking for a victim. The sun had set just a few minutes ago, and the rising moon illuminated the fountains below in a liquid, pale white.

The vamp slid in and out of the shadows, searching for an easy mark among the locals and tourists that gathered in the square. Some sat and drank wine, chatting with their neighbors, while others wandered, taking pictures or sight-seeing. The vampire must have thought he had gone completely unnoticed.

He was wrong.

Freddie had been watching him for days, ever since the grizzled, gaunt-looking American had stepped off the tube into King's Cross. He actually envied the guy's deep tan and dark brown locks. Freddie's bright red hair and pale skin made him stick out more in the moonlight.

Not that the man's coloring had kept him hidden. Freddie had spotted him almost immediately, the powerful scent of a newly made vampire drawing his attention, a rich bouquet of embers and ash.

There was something about the smell that brought out a melancholy in Freddie. It reminded him of the turbulent years after he'd been turned.

He didn't have a problem with rogue vampires. Some vamps weren't cut out for life in a coven. But you couldn't waltz into a new city and start feeding without checking in with the ruling power. If you came to London, you had to talk to Freddie's boss. That was just the way it was.

His master's Call tugged at him, filling him with an urgency to return. Freddie spoke an answer into his mind.

Soon. Dealing with a rogue.

Coven Master Hughes didn't respond in words, although Freddie felt a sort of amused grumbling come from him. Freddie's master knew he wouldn't keep him waiting without reason. Master Hughes trusted Freddie, as he should. Freddie had been the head of security for the Hughes Coven for decades now. He was devoted to his master and to his fellow vampires.

Freddie wasn't good at a lot of things. Small talk. Smiling. Making friends or, god forbid, finding lovers. But he kept people safe. Even if he often felt like an outsider among the other vampires, he would protect them until the last drop of his undead blood had been spilled. The Hughes Coven was his home, and he was its guardian.

A shift in the shadows, and the rogue was on the move. A tall, thin man in jeans and a ratty t-shirt, he was tailing a young blonde woman, probably college-age, as she made her way down the steps to the canal.

As the vampire closed in, she shivered and wrapped her jean jacket tighter around her, walking faster as she took the turn onto the path parallel to the waterway.

Despite his ragged appearance, the rogue vamp followed smoothly and confidently, sure of his ability to take down his victim.

He shouldn't have been so confident. Freddie moved like a ghost through the shadows, keeping just enough distance to stay unnoticed. He was in his element. He thrilled at the excitement of the hunt, filling with satisfaction that he was keeping the people of King's Cross safe, vampire and human alike.

"Slow down, little girl." The American stepped in front of the woman, and she jumped and stumbled back. Freddie had seen him coming with his heightened senses, but the rogue had moved too quickly for a normal human to follow.

"Who...what do you want?"

"Just to walk you home." The vampire closed the gap between them. Frozen in place, the woman's eyes darted around, searching for anyone else, but she was alone. The path was empty, a pale line running along the dark canal.

As the rogue vamp reached out, grabbing her arm and pulling her toward himself, Freddie was already there, his hand around the predator's neck.

The woman wrenched herself out of the rogue vampire's grasp.

"Go," Freddie growled at her. With a gasp, she took off running. Freddie didn't love to scare humans, he'd rather not be seen by them at all, but in situations like this, fear was a better motivator than some attempt at a logical explanation. He needed her gone so he could deal with the problem vamp struggling to escape his grip.

"Stop." Freddie glared at the rogue, letting his fangs drop. He lifted the vampire up by the neck. The interloper might be tall, but he couldn't compete with Freddie's six-foot-four frame and long limbs. The vamp squirmed as he kicked the empty air underneath him, clawing at Freddie's muscular arms and hissing.

Freddie's eyes narrowed. He preferred not to kill, but he would if he had to. The demon inside Freddie was moving under his skin, pushing for violence and blood. He didn't want to give into the urge, but he wouldn't have an intruder feeding in King's Cross.

"I'll break your neck," Freddie threatened. The vampire stilled, staring at him with arrogance and fear. Freddie loosened his grip enough to allow him to speak.

"Let me go." His words came out in a hoarse whisper.

"Where's your sire?" Freddie pitched his voice low, ensuring no humans further up the embankment would hear him.

The rogue pressed his lips together into a thin line, the tips of his fangs peeking out. His eyes narrowed. He didn't answer.

Freddie pulled him closer, their noses almost touching. "You smell, what, six months old?" he snarled. "Where's your sire?"

"He abandoned me," the vamp said. "In Tampa."

"You need to learn the rules." Freddie tossed the rogue to the ground. He gasped and forced air into his lungs. "Don't feed in King's Cross."

The vampire rose slowly from the earth, wiping off dirt and collecting himself. "Fine. Can I go?"

"No."

Freddie spun around and started back up toward Granary Square, gesturing for the vamp to follow.

"Where...where are we going?" The vamp's voice trembled. Freddie would have had more compassion if he hadn't just tried to feed on an innocent human.

"Come." Freddie took the stairs two at a time. Now that he'd captured the rogue vampire, he needed to get home. Master Hughes was waiting for him.

There was no sound of footsteps behind him. Freddie came to a stop. Why wouldn't rogues ever follow his instructions? If they did, they could travel freely through London. Check in with the coven house, refrain from feeding on humans. It was that simple. But no, they always had to run.

Freddie turned to look, and sure enough, the

rogue was gone. He scowled in annoyance. Why would a baby vamp think he could hide from a multicentenarian like Freddie? They tried his patience.

At an inhuman speed, Freddie flew down the path next to the canal. No infant vampire could outpace him. Even traveling that quickly, his eyes still spotted the flicker in the nearby copse of trees.

The rogue was on Freddie then, but he had lost the element of surprise. He let out a ferocious growl, his fangs and claws out, a whirlwind of movement, but Freddie was calm. The vamp had barely gotten a scratch in when he buried his own claws in the rogue's stomach.

He collapsed inward, Freddie's arm sticking rather grotesquely out of his guts as he rooted around inside. The rogue vampire screamed, high-pitched and desperate. Freddie's head began to throb. Why couldn't this ever be easy?

"Shut up." He pulled out his claw from the creature's bowels, bringing out his stomach and a good ten feet of intestine with it. The blood and viscera flowed down his forearm as he presented the vamp's organs to him. "We can keep going, if you want."

The vampire took one look at the bloody mess and passed out cold. Poor kid. Not that Freddie felt sorry for him, but he remembered what it was like to be so new, before violence and gore became a mundane part of daily life.

He let his trophy drop to the ground and hoisted the vamp over his shoulder. Everything about this had been inconvenient, but he was lucky it wasn't more serious. The rogue would heal up in a day or two, and hopefully, he'd be humble and compliant.

That's assuming that he had been planning to feed on the woman and not kill her. They'd find out once he was awake, and if tonight was to be the start of a killing spree, the outcome would be less pleasant for him.

There hadn't been a human death perpetrated by a vampire in London in decades. Freddie knew that was thanks to Master Hughes. It was one reason he admired him so much.

Once around the rooftops of King's Cross, the body of the vamp resting easily on his shoulder, and Freddie headed back to the coven house in Knightsbridge. The gold tips of the wrought-iron fence glistened in the moonlight, and the antique sconces on either side of the front door cast an amber glow over the white facade.

This had been Freddie's home for almost fifty years. He'd felt horribly out of place, joining a coven and moving in with so many other vampires. That hadn't fully gone away.

He recognized the strength of the community and worked to protect it, but he saw himself as an outsider. There was a camaraderie there that he couldn't seem to take part in. He had given up trying. Better to be the loner that's good at his job.

When he reached the main door, he nodded at Archie, an eager young vampire who'd joined only a month ago. Although Freddie hoped his puppyish enthusiasm would eventually wane over the ensuing decades, he would always have the face of a twenty-three-year-old grad student. Archie waved Freddie through enthusiastically.

"Welcome home, Lord Grosvenor."

Freddie grunted as he walked past. He hadn't been a Grosvenor in over two centuries.

"Grey, Archie. Freddie Grey."

No Grosvenor alive had any clue who he was. Archie was trying hard to impress. That wasn't an undesirable trait in a new coven member, as much as it might annoy him.

"Do you...do you want me to deal with that?" Archie scrunched his face in disgust, gesturing to the unconscious vampire slung over Freddie's shoulder.

"Please." In one easy motion, Freddie flipped the guy into Archie's arms. Archie held the rogue vamp away from himself like he was a rotting fish. Freddie nodded in thanks.

Freddie made his way up the stairs to the fifth floor, where Master Hughes' office and living quarters were located. The floorboards creaked as he ascended the levels of the old Georgian house. When he reached the top, he stopped in front of the heavy wooden door.

A jolt of anxiety kicked up, even after all these years. When Master Hughes first found him, Freddie had been a desperate, uncontrolled mess. He'd shown Freddie a different way to be, given him a home, and since then Freddie dearly wanted to prove that his trust had been well-placed.

He raised his fist to knock.

Come in, child.

Freddie hadn't been a child for centuries, but it wasn't condescending when Coven Master Hughes called him that. In many ways, he had taken the place of the biological father Freddie had lost when he became a vampire. And he'd certainly been more of a sire and guiding hand than the asshole that had made Freddie.

Freddie turned the brass handle and opened the door to the coven master's office. The furnishings had been carefully chosen, expensive but not over the top. Upon entering, your eye automatically went to the large mahogany desk that Master Hughes currently sat behind.

A handsome man who appeared to be in his early fifties, Master Hughes had perfect hair and a well-trimmed salt and pepper beard. He was fastidious about his appearance, and Freddie had never seen him look messy or disheveled.

Nearby, in a high-backed armchair, sat Daniel, the master's American husband. A lithe, blonde man, he bore the strong iron-and-ash scent of a new vampire.

Freddie didn't know Daniel very well, but he'd been impressed with how quickly the American had formed connections with the other vampires. Honestly, Freddie was jealous at how easily it came to him. There was a difficult contradiction between the wide-eyed overwhelm of a baby vampire and the authoritative presence needed to be coven master's mate, but Daniel had navigated it with grace.

It was unusual for him to be there. Freddie turned back to Master Hughes. His face was a still mask concealing a deep undercurrent of rage. The air crackled with it. Freddie couldn't recall another time he'd seen him so angry.

"Thank you for coming, my son. I have a job for you."

Freddie waited for more.

"It's the Azarians. They've threatened Daniel's nephew, Anthony."

Freddie frowned. The Azarians were all the way in New York, and there'd been some strain between the covens. They hadn't been willing to set down a proper treaty. Still, the Atlantic Ocean was wide. Freddie didn't understand what an American coven had to do with London vampires.

"Why?" Freddie asked.

"Anthony is an up-and-coming opera singer, a star tenor. He must have gained enough publicity to attract their attention, and they traced him back to Daniel and myself."

Freddie cocked his head. This still didn't make sense.

Master Hughes' eyes hardened. "The Azarians have been making veiled threats for some time now, blustering about the illegitimacy of our coven and attempting to forge alliances against us. They may be across the pond for the moment, but they have plans for expansion. Their imperialistic tendencies remind me of the dark times, back when the ancient ones used all as their pawns. I remember being caught between the armies of Enolf the Brute and Gabriela de Aragon. Charles Azarian seems to model himself after them."

"That's daft."

"It is, but ambition doesn't require intellect. Anthony needs a bodyguard until we can sort this out. I'd like you to do it."

Freddie hated the idea of being away. He could protect his coven-mates better than anyone, and he worried about leaving that job to someone less intelligent, or less ruthless. But if his master required it...

"Where?" Freddie asked.

Master Hughes glanced toward Daniel, who smiled, although it didn't reach his eyes, which were lined with worry and exhaustion.

"Anthony travels for his work, and his schedule is hectic. He's wrapping up in Chicago now, and you can meet him at his next engagement in San Francisco."

Freddie nodded, but he couldn't help scowling.

"I know you don't want to be away from the coven," Master Hughes continued. "You have always kept us all safe and hidden. In my estimation, the threat from the Azarians merits your presence. If they try to take him hostage, or worse, we will find ourselves in a vastly weakened position."

"I understand." Freddie pushed down his instinctual worry. The coven had many capable vampires to assume his duties. He needed to follow his master's wishes.

"Thank you," Daniel said, and lunged forward, hugging Freddie. It took everything in him to tamp down his instinctual, violent reaction. His master just looked amused.

Freddie hated hugs.

"He's like a son to me," Daniel said. Freddie could hear the tears threatening to spill out. Daniel stepped back, bringing himself under control. "He may not be happy that you're there. He's..."

"Self-obsessed." Master Hughes' voice was tinged with amusement.

"Oliver!"

"Let's not beat about the bush, my love. He is good at heart, but he doesn't concern himself with much outside of his own career ambitions. He's got blinkers on for everything else." Master Hughes turned back to Freddie. "He hasn't taken the danger seriously. Daniel didn't hear from him until he'd received a third letter."

Freddie rolled his eyes.

"I know. Not only that, but his first instinct was to get the police involved."

Freddie let out a low growl. Too many unfortunate run-ins with the authorities. Even those who knew about the existence of vampires often only had their own best interests in mind. To say that Freddie was wary of them would be a vast understatement.

"We're in agreement. You'll need to make sure Anthony doesn't involve them. More than that, he doesn't know that his uncle is a vampire. He has no idea about us at all, and we can't risk him finding out. I trust in your ability to manage his feelings as needed."

It was good Master Hughes was confident, because Freddie wasn't. He was at his best when he was alone on patrol, not when he was trying to persuade someone to act rationally. People skills were not his strength. Most days, he'd prefer not to speak at all.

Daniel looked up into Freddie's eyes. "You and I don't know each other very well, but...Anthony and my mother are the only family I have. Please take care of him."

Daniel's love for his nephew touched a deep part of Freddie. It made him think of his own family. The one he lost when he became a vampire, a mother and father that he loved. After the change, they had viewed him as a monster.

They weren't wrong.

"Freddie?" Daniel's voice brought him back to the present. "Are you okay?"

"I will protect him." Not only for Master Hughes' sake, but for Daniel's. He could see why his master loved the man so much. He had a sweet honesty and directness that could cut through any barriers one might erect.

"Thank you."

Freddie nodded and turned. He had to pack and book a flight. There was little time. Any moment he wasn't with Anthony was a moment when the man was in danger.

As he was heading down the stairs to his quarters, his master's voice whispered in his mind.

Freddie.

Sir?

I would have said this in person, but given vampire hearing, I thought it better to tell you mind-to-mind. Bernard is planning to retire as my First, sooner rather than later. You are under serious consideration to replace him.

Freddie stopped in his tracks. He was being considered for First?

I am honored sir...

But?

I'm not good with people. You know that.

I don't know that. What I know is, consciously or unconsciously, you keep yourself at a distance. I believe you can overcome that. Traveling outside of London will be positive for you, I think. Being around humans may teach you some things. Anthony is quite the handful.

That was ominous. Freddie brooded for a moment before Master Hughes continued.

Plus, who knows, perhaps you'll meet your mate out in the world somewhere.

Freddie stumbled as his foot missed the next step. His mate? He couldn't think of anything he would be less suited to than having a mate. Who would want to be saddled with a silent, brooding mess? Who would stand by him as his need for violence overtook him? Hell, with a mate to protect, his demon would be driving him to rampage, to give into the crimson surge at the slightest threat.

I'm not looking for that, Master.

Perhaps you should. You are not a mindless weapon, Freddie. You care about the vampires here. Show me you can be the First the coven needs.

As Master Hughes' presence left his mind, Freddie sighed in frustration. This whole thing promised to be both complicated and vague, two things that Freddie hated. As he reached the door to his room, he took a deep breath.

If Master Hughes believed he had it in him to be his First, then Freddie would do whatever it took to meet his master's expectations.

4

ANTHONY

ow the role of Ferrando from Mozart's *Cosí fan tutte* became one of Anthony's signatures, he'd never know. The character was not a great guy. Neither of the dudes in *Cosi* were.

Anthony hated the whole thing: making a bet on his fiancé's loyalty, wearing a disguise to trick said fiancé, all of it. But he was known for the part, and audiences loved the thing, so he was back in San Francisco.

Sometimes a new production would find a way to be more feminist, or at least more realistic, but not this one. Market Street Opera had been doing *this* production for the last twenty years. The costumes were dated and awful. The fake mustache for Anthony's disguise as an "Albanian" really pissed him off.

At least his big aria was pretty.

He tried to keep his spirits up as he unpacked his bags in the hotel room. The company had taken good care of him. The room was beautiful, with an eclectic mix of modern and antique touches, and the bathroom floor was heated, one of Anthony's favorite perks. And the bed...so cozy. If he had to do the creaky old opera at least he'd sleep comfortably.

He hung up the last of his shirts in the closet and fixed his hair in the mirror. He had *magnificent* hair, thick and brown from his Italian heritage, and although it was silly, he wouldn't leave without looking perfect. People expected it from him. He spritzed on Acqua di Gío and headed downstairs.

He walked into the restaurant. Hotel restaurants always had a decor that said "we're fancy, as long as you don't look too close." The fabric on the upholstered chairs might be suede, if you squinted, and the crown molding was barely holding on. One glance and Anthony saw that his date had not yet arrived.

His first instinct was annoyance. Don't schedule a nine a.m. appointment and no-show! Honestly, don't schedule a nine a.m. appointment at all. No matter. He took a deep breath and found the host. He just needed to have a cup of coffee.

Anthony sat down at the impeccably set table, careful not to bump into the man sitting nearby. He was a thin, ostentatiously dressed gentleman wearing a colorful, voluminous ascot around his neck.

The man squinted as Anthony squeezed by. He looked in his thirties and was reasonably attractive with smooth olive skin, but his style and demeanor were that of an elderly gay. He gave off a vibe much like the fussy men that attended Anthony's operas.

Anthony was stirring cream into his coffee when he spoke.

"Tea is better for the voice. Less dehydrating."

The words came out in a soft rasp. Anthony guessed it was the result of some sort of vocal injury. Anthony looked over his shoulder wearily. It was too early for a disgruntled opera lover.

"Are you a fan?"

"I wouldn't go that far, no. Just an admirer of...culture." The fancy man's eyes flashed, and for a moment, Anthony wondered if he'd offended him somehow.

"Well, that's lovely for you." Anthony turned back to his coffee.

"It is. I like to think I have refined taste. You should try it some time."

God, what a dick. Anthony was about to fling out some snarky retort when the general manager of the Market Street Opera entered the restaurant.

Rosemary Spooner was a tall, thin, formidable woman, the opera world's Miranda Priestly. When Anthony had worked here as a young artist, he'd been terrified of her, but he quickly learned that she ran the company like a tight ship, and if he did his job well, she'd keep giving him opportunities.

Anthony stood to shake her hand, smiling. "I love your Chanel suit, Rosemary. It's a classic."

"You're looking well, Anthony." Her face was still and calm. She sat, unfolding a napkin and laying it across her lap methodically. "You have quite the schedule this season."

"Strike while the iron is hot. Plus, I like traveling."

Rosemary squinted at him. "Where's your assistant? What's her name...Jennifer?"

Anthony sighed. "She's on vacation. For an entire

month." It was a sore subject. He dreaded being without her.

"When you're about to open an opera?"

"I couldn't say no." Anthony kneaded his forehead with his fingers. "She hasn't taken time off in two years."

Rosemary cocked her head and looked him up and down, assessing him. "Alright, out with it. Why are we here?"

"Breakfast with an old friend?" Anthony projected a flirtatious warmth. They'd always done this dance: he'd play coy, and she'd pull the truth out of him.

"Please, Anthony. I know you better than that. You don't socialize without an agenda."

"Call me *Antonio*."

Rosemary took a sip of her coffee. "I'm sorry?"

"In case anyone overhears."

"Everyone knows that you're from New Jersey."

"Not the European press."

"Good Lord." Rosemary rolled her eyes behind her thick but fashionable glasses.

"I *could* have been born in Italy, rather than being third generation." Anthony winked at her. "Just trying to stay mysterious."

"What do you need from me, *Antonio*?"

Anthony steeled himself. This would test how far his newfound influence might take him. Rosemary was a shrewd negotiator.

"I hate the production."

"Of *Così fan tutte*? Of course you do. Everyone hates it, except for the elderly subscribers who have been watching it for the last four decades."

"I'm contracted to do it again in three years."

Rosemary pressed her lips together. "You are."

"I want a new production."

Rosemary raised an eyebrow. "Or...?"

"Or I bail. I'm trying to phase out the role, anyway. *Cenerentola* is earlier that season. I don't need to come back twice."

Rosemary barked out a laugh. "Nobody comes to *Così* for the Ferrando, no matter how many times the reviewers call it an ensemble piece. The ladies are the stars."

"Then it won't be a big deal for me to skip it."

A tense silence settled between them. Anthony was suddenly very aware of the man behind him with the ascot. He was clinking his spoon against a ceramic mug as he stirred what Anthony assumed was tea.

Finally, Rosemary shrugged. "Fine. It was time for a new production."

"Excellent!"

"But." She raised her finger imperiously. "The

season after, you'll do *Don Giovanni*."

"Ugh. Don Ottavio is such a simp."

"If you didn't want to play lightweights, you should have been born with a heftier instrument."

Anthony sighed dramatically, his hand going to his forehead. "My curse." He'd gotten what he wanted. Mostly. He could afford to joke.

"I'll have Melissa send over the—"

"Oh my god, Antonio Bianchi! I love you!" The high-pitched call echoed off the tiled ceiling of the hotel restaurant. Rosemary and Anthony both turned their heads toward the shrill voice.

A young blonde woman rushed over to their table, trailed by a bald, tattooed man in his mid-thirties. Her long hair had a crispy, over-processed quality, and she wore a deep plum lipstick. He had a goatee that made him look like a comic book villain.

"Hello." It might be inconvenient sometimes, but Anthony didn't really mind his more rabid fans, especially when they were younger than seventy. It was a sign his career was doing well. He plastered on a big smile.

"Could I get an autograph?" Her eyes were bright with excitement. The bald man behind her wore a deep scowl.

"Anything for a fan." Anthony looked around.

Without a word, Rosemary reached in her bag and handed him a notepad and a very expensive-looking brown and gold pen.

"What's your name?"

"Hannah," the woman answered. She kept playing with the curls of her long blonde hair. "Oh my god, my mother is going to die. She loves you *so much*, she's been an opera fanatic forever. She says you're the next Pavarotti."

"That's very kind of her." Anthony scrawled *Keep music in your heart, cara Hannah* on the paper and signed it, handing it over.

"Wait. I'm having breakfast with her in fifteen minutes. It's only four blocks away. You *have* to come with."

"She seems very sweet, but I'm already having—"

"She'd be so mad at me if I didn't bring you. Come on." Hannah tugged on Anthony's arm. Her wild look ignited a shock of anxiety in him.

"Please don't pull on me. I can't—"

"I told you, you *have* to!" Hanna was pulling hard, and Anthony wrenched his arm away with a jerk.

"You can't—"

"If my girlfriend says you're coming, you're coming." The gruff voice startled Anthony. It was Goatee.

He stepped closer, looming over Anthony. His

loose t-shirt revealed a hint of a muscular frame underneath. Anthony glanced back at Rosemary. She was texting furiously, her face blank. He hoped she was telling her assistant to call the police.

Anthony suddenly felt very small. He had never been a fighter. "I'm sorry, I—"

"Now." The man lifted him off the chair in a rough grip. He squeezed *hard*, his fingers digging into Anthony's skin. Anthony struggled to maintain his balance as he came to standing.

"Thanks baby, you always take care of me." Hannah stroked the man's arm, but he didn't take his eyes off Anthony.

"Move, unless you want me to break something." He pushed, and Anthony stumbled forward. Shit, this guy was strong. This was worse than any creepy fan he'd encountered so far. He was actually starting to get scared.

"Please, I just—"

With a crash, Goatee's body hit the adjacent table, the wood splintering under his weight. The gentleman in the ascot managed to rescue his tea without missing a beat, holding it above his head with an annoyed expression on his face.

Anthony spun around and was confronted by the sight of a tall, muscular man in a black suit. He had short red hair and striking, angular cheekbones, with a hint of the feral in his eyes. He stood in a defensive stance, presumably in case the bald boyfriend got up off the floor.

Anthony couldn't get his mouth to make words. That was new.

The redheaded man nodded at him, not breaking his position. The blonde fan launched herself at baldie, who was still conscious but was looking fairly dazed.

"Baby, are you okay? Did they hurt you?"

The boyfriend murmured something to her, his gaze darting to Anthony's ginger savior. Without saying another word, he hobbled off, leaning on his girlfriend for support. Anthony barely noticed them leaving. He was staring at the besuited man's broad shoulders and deep blue eyes.

"And who might you be?" Rosemary asked, casually spreading butter onto a scone.

Anthony still couldn't speak.

"Bodyguard, ma'am." His voice was low, rumbling around in his chest as he spoke, and he pronounced the word 'ma'am' as 'mum.' Dammit, he was British. That just wasn't fair.

"Thank goodness. Fans can be aggressive, even for a so-called 'dead' art form. At a certain level, getting security is wise. Very smart, Anthony."

Anthony looked back and forth between them. What the hell was happening?

"Anthony's looking a bit pale, Mr....?"

"Freddie."

"Indeed. Why don't you take him upstairs to his room, Freddie? He could probably use a rest after all the excitement."

Anthony nodded.

"Beautiful. I'll stay and finish my scone. See you at rehearsal tomorrow."

Freddie gestured for Anthony to walk in front of him. Anthony moved forward on shaky legs, wondering if he was now going to his room with a serial killer. Some flaws, even a gorgeous face and a perfect body couldn't overcome.

As the elevator ascended, Anthony breathed deeply and regained the power of speech. "Listen, I don't know—"

The elevator door opened and Freddie held up his hand to quiet him. Anthony rolled his eyes. All this spy stuff was a pile of baked bullshit. He stepped out and took a right.

Freddie cleared his throat. "Wrong way."

Anthony had arrived a few hours ago. He couldn't be expected to remember where his room was. He trailed behind Freddie in the other direction.

How had he known? When they reached Anthony's room, Freddie waved a card and the door unlocked. He opened it.

"What the hell?" Anthony was unable to control the trepidation in his voice. How had Freddie gotten a key?

Freddie shrugged. Shooting him the look of death, Anthony stepped into the door frame, and was immediately stopped by Freddie's arm across his chest. It was a nice arm. Anthony felt the solid muscle against his torso, even through the suit jacket.

"Let me."

Freddie gestured for him to wait and went in. Anthony stood awkwardly, staring helplessly as Freddie checked the closet and disappeared into the bathroom.

Every second he spent waiting in the hall, he got angrier and angrier. Who the hell did this guy think he was? Even if his accent *was* fucking perfect, he had no right to order Anthony around.

Freddie stuck his head out.

"Okay."

Anthony stormed through the entryway, facing off with Freddie as the door slammed shut behind him.

"I didn't hire you."

"Your uncle did." Freddie's tone was even, and his

face betrayed no emotion.

"Uncle Danny hired you? I don't believe you. He wouldn't know how to find someone like you."

"Master Hughes has many connections."

"Master Hughes? You mean Oliver?"

"Yes. I go where he sends me."

"I don't believe you," Anthony repeated. He pulled out his cell phone and hit Daniel's name. Freddie crossed to the window and pushed the curtain to the side, surveying the streets below.

"Hi sweetie!" His uncle's voice was cheerful, but Anthony pegged it as fake. It was the tone Daniel took when he had done something he shouldn't have, like the time he'd called the high school to complain when Anthony hadn't gotten the lead in *Anything Goes*.

"Uncle Danny, did you get me a bodyguard?"

"Aww, you only call me Uncle Danny when you're angry."

"Well, I am! Did you or did you not hire someone to be my bodyguard?" His uncle wasn't going to wriggle out of this one.

"Oliver and I were worried about you, honey. We knew Freddie would be right for the job."

"I can't have a bodyguard!"

"Just until this whole stalking thing dies down."

Danny's voice had a hint of genuine fear in it. Anthony could be compassionate about that later.

"It was only a few letters," Anthony said. "I'll call the cops or something, get a restraining order. I won't be saddled with some creepy meathead."

"You can't get a restraining order when you don't know who the stalker is. And Oliver says Freddie saved you from an aggressive fan, so they aren't the only problem."

"How the hell does Oliver know that?" Anthony glared at Freddie, who was still staring out the window, his face blank. "It just happened a couple of minutes ago."

"Freddie checks in regularly."

"So not only is he intruding on my space, he's reporting back to you two on my life?"

"He's there to keep you safe."

"I don't need that!"

"Please, Tony, for me?"

"Don't call me that. I'm not a teenager anymore. You can't saddle me with some muscle-bound shadow."

Anthony hung up and threw his phone on the bed. This was ridiculous. His uncle had always been overprotective, but this was too far.

"Creepy meathead?"

Anthony startled. Freddie's deep baritone sent a

shiver down his spine. His body's unconscious response infuriated him.

Sure, Freddie's voice was rumbly and sexy, and sure, he was tall, and his skin was porcelain with the perfect scattering of freckles. And sure, his hair was a truly rare shade of red. It didn't matter. He would not be charmed by this British lunk.

"I stand by it."

Freddie shrugged and sat down in the office chair aside the tinker toy table the hotel considered a desk.

"What are you doing?" Anthony asked, his voice rising higher in pitch than he would have liked. "You're not staying."

Freddie said nothing.

"You are *not* my bodyguard. I didn't hire you. Get out of my room!"

Freddie still said nothing.

"I said, get out!" Anthony grabbed the phone from the nightstand. "I'm calling hotel security."

"Why?"

"Because you're a stranger and you're in my room and you won't leave!"

"What will you tell them?"

"That my uncle hired a bodyguard for me against my will and he won't get out and he attacked a fan of mine in the restaurant..." As the words left his lips and hit the cold air of the hotel room, Anthony trailed off. It did seem ridiculous.

Freddie's face was a still mask as he positioned himself to keep tabs on the outside of the hotel and have a conversation at the same time.

Anthony was losing the steam of his righteous indignation. "I don't want you here."

"I know."

"So leave."

"No."

Anthony sank down onto the soft mattress of the bed. This was absolutely ludicrous. He didn't need a bodyguard, and he certainly didn't need this near-mute monstrosity hanging around him all the time. He hated tall people. They made everyone else feel inadequate.

He would have to convince his uncle to call Freddie off. He'd find a way to show Daniel that everything was fine. God. How was he able to screw up Anthony's life from over five thousand miles away? He was sweating just thinking about it.

He shook it off and stood up.

"Where are you going?"

Anthony shot him the coldest stare he could muster. "I'm going to use the toilet. Then, I'm taking a shower. This whole thing has got me feeling gross."

Anthony slammed the bathroom door closed

behind him. He leaned against the thick wood. At least he had something solid between himself and this frustrating intrusion in his life. What a nightmare.

5

FREDDIE

Anthony turned on the water, and Freddie sighed with relief. He desperately needed a moment to himself. Anthony was everything he hated about being around people. He was loud, demanding, and obnoxious.

Master Hughes and Daniel had warned Freddie, but he hadn't really understood how difficult this would be. Anthony could make his job impossible. Why did he have to be so stubborn?

And why did he have to smell so good? After hundreds of years of heightened senses, Freddie no longer registered the scent of the typical human he ran across in daily life. He noticed only when something was seriously wrong, when the odor of decay was strong enough to attract his attention. He couldn't remember the last time he'd caught the aroma of any man, never mind one so pleasant.

Anthony smelled more than pleasant. He smelled *delicious*, a mix of citrus and leather, both fresh and well-worn. Freddie wanted to lick him from head to toe. And he was exactly Freddie's type: short and solid, with olive skin and dark eyes, like a young Stanley Tucci, but with a better ass.

Anthony stood just beyond the door, slowly removing his clothes piece by piece. Freddie couldn't help but imagine it, Anthony unbuttoning his shirt to reveal a layer of fine brown hair. Were his nipples tiny, barely big enough to flick his tongue against, or were they larger? Large enough to suck hard, as Anthony writhed and moaned beneath him.

He'd have to unbutton his pants. He couldn't slide them down over that gorgeous ass. Freddie saw it in his mind's eye: his hands cupping those firm cheeks, grabbing onto those muscular thighs. And his cock? There's no way it wasn't beautiful. Everything about him was beautiful.

Why was he so fixated? He'd just met the man. He spent the last hundred years ignoring humans. Yet this one human, this one frustrating man, he captivated Freddie's imagination. He'd known him for all of an hour, but his inner demon was humming with electricity, not slumbering as it usually did. Even the monster inside of him wanted a taste.

The sound of feet against tile reached Freddie's ears as Anthony stepped into the shower. He couldn't keep the image from his mind: Anthony covering himself in soap, letting the water run down his toned body, forming rivulets in his fine chest hair.

He shook his head, throwing off the seductive vision that had taken up residence there. What was wrong with him? He moved to the far corner of the hotel room, away from the bathroom. Maybe a little distance would allow him to focus.

That's when it began: the soft slap of water and skin. Freddie cursed his vampire abilities, the superpowered senses that let him know exactly what was happening. Anthony was jerking off. Why would he do that? Was he trying to torture Freddie?

The slightest moan floated through the closed bathroom door, and Freddie was hard, so hard it was painful. He felt himself strain against the fabric of his tight suit pants. This was ridiculous! Freddie was a two-hundred-year-old vampire, not some schoolboy with a classroom hard-on.

The slapping sound came faster now, and Freddie couldn't help but imagine Anthony, his cock in his fist, his smooth fingers running back and forth down the shaft, teasing the head. Did he shudder with the intensity of his need? Was he leaning, one hand against the shower wall and one hand wrapped around his erection?

That's when the stifled moans began, wordless at first. Freddie's vision blurred with his body's reaction to the sound. Anthony's voice, too soft to be heard by human ears, teased him. He shifted his hard-on, trying to ease the painful restriction.

"Mmm...mmmm...yes...please...suck me..."

It was too much. Freddie was trembling, Anthony's expressions of ecstasy hitting him deep at his core. They came fast and furious now.

"Yes...please...that's it...oh fuck...oh fuck......"

And then a final word, mumbled so softly that even with his supernatural hearing, Freddie wasn't certain of what he heard.

"...Freddie..."

With the sound of his name, real or imagined, Freddie's vision flashed with a bright white light. His fangs dropped, not in his control, piercing the flesh of his bottom lip. And his whole body shook as the orgasm took him, desperate relief flowing over him.

The tremors continued as the smell of Anthony's release hit his nose, sweet and citrus. The powerful scent overwhelmed Freddie's senses, tempting him and enticing him through the door. Freddie looked down at himself.

Shit.

It finally registered that he had come in his pants. Thank god he was in a black suit, the wet stain was barely visible. Still, it was embarrassing, and more than that, it was utterly ridiculous.

Why would he have this reaction? He was on the job. They had just met. Had he been so desperate for a sensual connection that his body had taken over?

He pushed down his humiliation and buttoned his suit coat. Hopefully, that would help cover the signs of what had happened. He could consider any deeper meaning later. Or maybe never. He didn't need to think about Anthony and his strong thighs and his perfect ass—

Freddie.

He blinked his eyes, erasing the image of Anthony from his brain and searching for something to replace it. Dead puppies, the taste of cilantro, the sound of the word moist, anything to prevent Master

Hughes from catching him imagining Anthony naked.

Sir?

You're flustered.

Sorry, sir. Having a look around the hotel room. Master Hughes would know if Freddie was lying mind-to-mind, but maybe he would let it pass this time.

You've spent some time with Anthony then.

A few minutes.

I've only met him once, at my wedding, but he struck me as intelligent, charismatic, and a massive pain.

Accurate, sir. The water turned off in the bathroom.

How are you getting along?

We're not. He's angry. I've made it clear he's stuck with me.

There was a pause. Freddie felt his master's attention split. He was probably speaking to someone. Anthony's hair dryer blared from behind the bathroom door.

Daniel says you have to wear him down. Anthony is stubborn, but he can be persuaded. Daniel suggests that you seduce him.

What? Freddie's brain short-circuited as Master Hughes' words crashed up against his lustful thoughts from earlier.

Evidently, he's susceptible to flattery. You don't have to sleep with him if you'd rather not. Freddie started, then heard the rumble of Master Hughes' laugh in his mind. *Oh, come now, you're one of my lieutenants. You can't hide such a powerful emotion from me.*

He's handsome.

Of course he is, as are you. It's a good pairing.

It's a job.

This is a vampire coven, Freddie, not a Fortune 500 company. There's no HR department.

Freddie didn't answer. He wished Master Hughes would move on from his line of thinking.

Keep your integrity, if you feel that strongly. I wouldn't have it any other way. Let me know if you need anything.

Very well, sir.

As his coven master's presence left his mind, the door to the bathroom opened and Anthony stepped out. A towel was wrapped around his waist.

Freddie swallowed, and his throat tightened. Fine, dark hair covered Anthony's chest, just as Freddie had imagined, and his pecs were surprisingly well-defined. Freddie fought to prevent his eyes from following Anthony's furry treasure trail down lower.

"I've decided what to do."

Anthony was trying to project authority, but the fact that he was nearly naked made the whole thing cute. Freddie waited, one eyebrow raised.

"My uncle may have set this up, but I shouldn't have to deal with you. I won't tell you where I'm going or what I'm doing. You can figure it out on your own. And you can't sleep in my room. I'm not going to switch rooms to get you a bed."

"I can sleep in the armchair." Freddie didn't ever need sleep, but Anthony couldn't know that.

"No. I don't want you watching me at night, and you can't be around when I bring someone back to my hotel room."

"No guests."

"What?!" Anthony's face flushed with frustration. "That is not okay. I'm not going to let you—"

"No guests. It's not safe." Freddie sat back down in the wheeled office chair. He guessed that he should find Anthony's anger annoying, but it mostly struck him as adorable. He liked that the man had a big personality and strong opinions, but he was throwing himself against a brick wall. Freddie wasn't going to budge.

And he sure as hell wouldn't wait outside while Anthony fucked a stranger. His fangs tingled at the thought of it.

"This is ridiculous! All because of a few stupid letters!" Anthony went to the dresser and pulled out a pair of underwear, putting them on underneath the towel. He tossed the wet cloth back on the bathroom floor and threw on a white t-shirt.

Now Freddie had a full view of Anthony's bulge in his navy blue boxer shorts. His mouth watered.

Freddie blinked, bringing his focus back to the problem at hand. Anthony continued to rant as he dressed.

"This is an absolute travesty. I will *not* have my social life ruined because of some extortion scam or something. I'm not going to speak to you. I'm not going to look at you. You don't exist."

"That won't work." Freddie thrilled a little at poking back at him. He didn't know if it would help his cause, but he loved the look on Anthony's face when he goaded him.

"I don't care. I'm not dealing with you." Anthony slipped on a pair of very tight jeans and was tucking himself into them. Freddie moved toward him and did something completely out of character: he flirted.

"I'll be here." Freddie pitched his voice low. "I'm not going anywhere. You'll talk to me. You'll do what I tell you to do. I'll keep you safe."

Anthony's eyes went wide, and Freddie could smell his arousal, even so soon after coming. They stood like that, their faces a few inches apart, for a minute or maybe longer. Finally, Anthony managed to wrench himself away.

"We'll see."

6

ANTHONY

"**What the hell are you doing here?"**

"Is that any way to greet an old friend?" Lena smirked at Anthony, her makeup and hair perfect as always, looking ridiculously glamorous for a morning rehearsal. Anthony envied how effortless his friend's style was. He always looked perfect as well, of course, but it took hours of maintenance to make it happen.

"I thought Elisa was the Fiordiligi." Elisa Sinclair was a mezzo-soprano that had gone through the Young Artist's Program at Market Street at the same time as Anthony. She and Anthony got along well, although she was somewhat *approximate* when it came to pitch.

"She's been having vocal problems," Lena said, shrugging.

"So she finally admitted it? When I did *Roberto Devereaux* in Berlin last year, she took two full acts to warm up."

"She pulled out a few weeks ago. I had a gap in my schedule, so you're stuck with me."

"We'll all just have to suffer through your version of '*Come scoglio.*'" Anthony's sarcasm didn't have any real ire in it. As nosy and pushy as Lena was, Anthony appreciated he could trust her on stage. If something went wrong, she'd fix it and move on without breaking a sweat.

"Who's the handsome drink of water over there?" Lena gestured to a chair in the far corner, where Freddie sat, a scowl on his pale, freckled face. Somehow, he looked both prickly and appealing.

Anthony couldn't stop from frowning. It was bad enough Freddie had to follow him around. Did he have to make an eyesore of himself?

"My bodyguard."

Lena stared at him. "What?"

"I've been getting some...letters. Someone's been leaving them in my hotel rooms? My uncle took matters into his own hands."

"Why didn't you tell me?" Lena's face grew serious. "What did they say?"

"Barely anything." Anthony waved his hand dismissively. "They've just been vaguely threatening. My uncle overreacted."

"But they've been breaking into your hotels? I think your uncle reacted the exact right amount."

"I'm not worried about the letters, I'm worried about *him*. I should have just filled out a restraining order or something. Instead, I'm saddled with that wet blanket. It's been four days, and he's always around. He sleeps in my room, he won't leave me alone, and he's putting a dent in my love life. I tried to bring back this personal trainer that I met at the gay grocery store, and Freddie wouldn't let him through the door!"

Lena rolled her eyes. "You can take a breather, you know." She glanced over at the muscular bodyguard. "His name's Freddie, huh? Why go out looking when you've got that at home?"

"Are you kidding me?" Anthony grasped at a string of imaginary pearls around his neck.

"What, you don't like redheads? Who also happen to be handsome and tall and muscle-y enough to break you in half?"

"He's a security guard, for Christ's sake. He says five words at a time, if you're lucky, and he beats people up for a living." Anthony put on his best poker face. "Besides, he's not that handsome."

"I'm so sorry, a quiet, broody, tall redhead who probably has a crazy good body underneath that suit isn't enough for you? You could cut glass on that jaw."

"Keep it down," Anthony whispered. "I don't want him to know we're talking about him."

"Why not?" Lena raised an eyebrow with a mischievous twinkle.

"Because! It's bad enough I have to deal with his whole controlling bodyguard act. It'll be a thousand times worse if he knows...if he thinks that I'm attracted to him."

Lena reached out and squeezed Anthony's arm. "He's smoking hot. He's *right there* in your hotel room. Take him to pound town. Give him the Tony Bianchi special."

"This is silly." Anthony looked down and away. He wished he hadn't told Lena as much as he had.

"Bone him, Anthony."

"You're just trying to make up for your dull love life by living vicariously through me."

"I am!" Lena made grabby motions with her hands. "Feed mama! I want details!"

Anthony held up a hand to quiet her. "He's a macho bodybuilder type working in security. There's no chance in hell that he's gay."

"He might be bi. Why don't you find out?"

"Because I'm going to ignore him until he goes away."

Lena started to respond when the conductor cleared his throat. Anthony was thankful to end that awkward conversation. Soon enough, he had lost himself in the music, letting Mozart work his magic as the other leads joined Lena and himself in a soaring quartet.

The rehearsal flew by. Once it was done, Anthony gathered his things and started toward the door. Freddie strode over from across the room, matching Anthony's pace as he traveled down the hall.

"Plans?"

Anthony ignored him. He'd said he wouldn't engage, and he meant it. Freddie didn't press the issue, staying by his side as he got into the elevator. They didn't speak as the lift lowered them to the ground floor at a painfully slow rate.

Freddie broke the silence. "You sounded good."

Anthony's face warmed, and he knew he was blushing, which was ridiculous. People had been complimenting his voice since he was a teenager. This was no different. He didn't respond.

Freddie continued without making eye contact. "You looked at home."

Why was Freddie being nice? His voice was as gruff as always, but this was almost…sweet?

Anthony shook it off. It didn't matter that he was attractive, and it didn't matter that he was being nice. He was a huge inconvenience. It might not be his fault that he'd been assigned to Anthony, but that didn't mean Anthony had to make it easy for him.

Without saying a word, Anthony took a right, walking southwest on Market Street. He wouldn't brief Freddie every time he wanted to go somewhere. The bodyguard didn't comment, keeping pace in silence. A trolley rumbled by them, like the deep roll of timpani in an orchestra, providing a contrast to the quiet between them.

It wasn't long before they hit one of San Francisco's famous hills, and Anthony was breathing heavily as they climbed. He glanced over at Freddie, who hadn't broken a sweat. Anthony had assumed that Freddie would be in better shape than him, considering all those muscles, but Freddie looked infuriatingly relaxed. He could have been a prince on a litter. The exertion hadn't affected him at all.

By the time they reached the top of the first hill, Anthony couldn't hide his labored breathing. He bent over at the waist, hands on his hips. Frustration filled him. He was a professional opera singer! Breath control was his whole thing. Not only was Freddie unaffected, but Anthony looked like a shiny, sweaty pumpkin in front of the annoyingly fit bodyguard.

Which was silly. Why should he care what he looked like? Freddie was a hired hand. He didn't give a shit that Anthony's skin had expelled enough perspiration to solve the California water crisis.

Freddie crossed his arms, looking down on the city from the top of the hill. "Taxi?" he asked.

Anthony frowned but said nothing. He took a deep breath and started down the hill. Freddie shrugged and stayed beside him. It was like he was taunting Anthony with how easy this was for him. Jerk.

Up and down a few more hills, and Anthony's shirt soaked through. Freddie was as dry as a bone. Anthony was moving from annoyed to confused.

These were some killer hills, and Freddie was totally nonchalant about it. He hadn't even taken off his suit jacket.

"The Castro?" Freddie asked as gay pride flags and window decals appeared in the shops they were passing.

Anthony nodded. "Yeah. If you're worried about catching the gay, go back to the hotel room."

Freddie snorted. The two of them strolled through the streets of the old neighborhood, watching the shops and the people going about their daily lives. It struck Anthony how very different his life was from that of the folks here.

"I like coming here," he said, suddenly wanting to fill the silence. "Feeling the connection to history. The gay forefathers or something."

A man and woman in their twenties were coming towards them. The man was pushing a navy blue double-wide stroller. It took up the whole sidewalk. They were oblivious to the fact that Anthony and Freddie had to squeeze against the brick wall of a storefront to get out of the way.

Anthony glanced back as they continued on their way. "There are a lot more straight people here than when I was a young artist. Which is fine, I guess. Things change."

"They do. You can't stop it." Freddie looked sad suddenly, and Anthony had the impulse to reach out and touch him, to run his hand down one of those muscular arms in comfort.

He stopped himself. He wasn't even supposed to be talking to Freddie! Freddie smirked at him. Anthony looked away, locking his eyes straight ahead as they continued along.

Without intending it, they found themselves at one of Anthony's favorite spots in the Castro, the Vulcan Stairs. The steps stretched up in front of them, the greenery forming two walls on either side and giving it a calm, secluded feel even in the middle of the crowded city. The thick leaves muffled the sound of traffic, the birds chirping to fill in the absence.

Anthony's stomach churned. He loved the Vulcan Stairs, but it was odd to be here with someone else. Alone, the place was a meditative sanctuary amidst the busy bustle of San Francisco. In the company of another person, the place felt almost romantic. He did not want that experience with Freddie.

This was ridiculous. Freddie had been with him for four days and he was already cramping his style. Anthony wouldn't let his red-headed albatross stop him. He started up the stairs, moving ahead of Freddie, pretending that he was alone.

Soon enough, he was breathing heavily again. He was taking the stairs faster than he normally would, trying to stay in front of the ever-present bodyguard.

"You are ruining everything!" Anthony stopped and gasped for air as he reached a landing.

Freddie stepped up next to him. He said nothing, of course, but he wore a compassionate expression. It stoked Anthony's anger even further. He didn't need Freddie's pity!

"I didn't want a bodyguard. Now I can't enjoy one of my favorite places in the city because I've got you trailing behind me. It's not fair."

"I'm sorry?" Confusion flashed across Freddie's face, and something else. Had Anthony hurt him? Two warring emotions burned in Anthony's gut. He was furious that he had to deal with this, but underneath that, he wanted Freddie to stop looking wounded, to go back to his impenetrable, stony neutral.

Anthony sighed, releasing some of his rage. "It's not your fault. It's whoever is sending those stupid letters, and Uncle Danny for being so overprotective. Although maybe it is your fault because you could have just left once you realized I didn't want you here. I don't want any of this!"

Tears welled up in Anthony's eyes. He hadn't realized how overwhelmed he was. Underneath the facade, he was actually freaked out by everything that had happened. He'd been hiding that even from himself.

The loss of freedom exacerbated the issue. There's nothing Anthony treasured as much as agency over his own life. Since he was old enough to understand the death of his parents, he'd committed to forging his own path, to not being at the mercy of the world around him. Now that was being taken from him. It was all too much.

Freddie stepped closer, his eyes connecting with Anthony's. There was compassion there, but also something burning underneath.

7

ANTHONY

"You're okay."

With those two soft words, something gave way inside of Anthony. He looked at Freddie for the first time, really looked, and saw that Freddie wasn't just a brick wall to bash his head against. There was a possibility that the brick might form a solid foundation.

Without thinking, he leaned into Freddie. Freddie froze, and Anthony's heart pulsed with anxiety. Had he misread the situation? Had he crossed a line?

"I'm...I'm sorry..." Anthony moved away.

Freddie's powerful arms wrapped around him, keeping him in place, holding him in the most solid of embraces. Freddie was cool against him, a balm for his overheated emotions. He looked up at Freddie's face. It was open and unguarded. Anthony hadn't expected that.

Anthony was not used to being comforted. He wasn't sure if he liked it. He liked to be the most competent person in the room, the one who was calm and collected, the one who couldn't be fucked with. But having Freddie pressed against him, being held tight to Freddie's chest, some knot of worry and fear had released. Anthony was fully at ease for the first time in a long time.

And so fucking turned on. He could feel Freddie growing hard against him, and his own body responded. Anthony looked up to see the softness in Freddie's face turn sharp with desire. Butterflies stirred in Anthony's stomach.

"Kiss me," Anthony whispered.

"Anthony..."

"Please." Anthony heard how desperate he sounded, but he didn't care. Freddie looked down at him, and his face flashed with indecision. For a moment, Anthony thought he would say no, but then Freddie ran his tongue over his lips and bent down.

He was gentle at first, his soft, warm lips grazing Anthony's. It was sweet, careful and caring in a way Anthony hadn't expected, belying the image of the musclebound brute Anthony had in his mind.

It was too sweet. Anthony pressed forward, needing more, desperate to deepen the kiss.

Freddie responded in kind, more urgent now, his tongue running along Anthony's bottom lip. Anthony opened his mouth and Freddie's tongue entered him, flicking and licking inside his mouth, searching and teasing. Freddie was strong, but he kissed with a coyness that was sexy as hell. Anthony closed his eyes as he lost himself in the warmth.

"You two should get a room."

Freddie spun around, shoving Anthony behind him. In front of them stood three men. Two of them wore leather and tight black jeans, their cuffed up pant legs revealing the shine of combat boots. They looked young, in their twenties, if that. The one in the middle was older and was bald with a goatee and a neck tattoo. There was something familiar about him.

"Have I died and gone to a biker convention?" Anthony couldn't stop himself. They looked straight out of central casting. "Or some alternative timeline where everyone dresses like a greaser?"

The middle one's eyes flashed with anger. "You're one to talk. Your hair's stiff enough to cut glass."

At the sound of his gruff voice, Anthony recognized who he was.

"You!" The words burst out of him as the realization hit him. "You're the asshole boyfriend who grabbed me at the hotel restaurant!"

"You're coming with us," Goatee said. "My master has business with you."

"No, he doesn't." Freddie clenched and unclenched his fists, keeping himself as a barrier between Anthony and the threatening men. Anthony didn't know what the hell they were up to, and he knew he should be scared, but he wasn't. Maybe it was Freddie, tall and muscular and strong, protecting him. Anthony hated feeling weak, but he was no fighter, and seeing Freddie standing there like a shield made his skin tingle with excitement.

"This doesn't concern you, *bloke*," one of the others chimed in. "Go back to London, where you belong."

Freddie said nothing, but Anthony could feel the rage pouring off of him.

"You know these guys?" Anthony asked. "Who the hell are they? Who is their 'master'?"

"Someone who could cause you a lot of pain if you don't do as we say." Goatee was trying to act macho, but all three of them were eyeing Freddie with caution. They spread out a little, taking fighting stances.

"Freddie?" Anthony figured Freddie could handle himself, but it was three against two. Three against one, really, since Anthony hadn't been in a single fistfight in his entire life.

"They're no one," Freddie answered.

"We'll see about that." Goatee gestured toward Freddie and Anthony, and the two toughs that flanked him moved towards them.

The one on the left swung at Freddie. It came fast and furious, and Anthony flinched, certain that Freddie would be hit in the face. But Freddie dodged it, and kicked the kid right in the sternum, sending him flying back.

The one on the right was on Freddie then, not looking back at the other punk splayed out on the ground. As he closed the distance, Freddie elbowed him in the jaw, and he stumbled back, dazed. He tripped over an uneven cobblestone and fell on his ass.

"Brian! What the hell?" The first one, having recovered enough to sit up, looked to Goatee for help.

"Brian? Your name is Brian?" Anthony asked. "Seriously? How mundane can you get?"

"There's nothing wrong with my name!" Goatee, or Brian rather, yelled back.

Anthony laughed, unable to help himself. "Doesn't exactly strike fear, you know?"

"You're lucky you have your little bodyguard," Brian growled, stepping forward. "Not that it matters. We can take him."

Freddie shifted his weight back and forth between his legs in his protective stance. "Those idiots are too young," he said to the bald vampire. "They're weak from the sun."

What the hell did that mean? They did look twenty-ish, but Anthony didn't understand what the sun had to do with it.

"I don't need them," Brian said. "I can handle you."

Freddie chuckled, and the low, resonant sound made Anthony's balls tingle. Jesus Christ. Could he turn off the lust for one second? They were in a fight!

Freddie cocked his head, considering the man in front of him. Brian was in shape. He had some muscles, but he was small compared to Freddie.

"No," Freddie said. "I don't think you can."

Brian hissed at them, actually *hissed*, and lunged for Freddie. He moved so fast that for a second, Anthony thought he saw him blur. Except that wasn't possible.

"Freddie!"

Anthony yelped as Brian's fist connected with Freddie's stomach. It was a killer punch, with his entire strength behind it, and it landed square on.

Freddie didn't even flinch. Before Anthony could blink, Freddie punched the bald man right in the jaw. Brian stumbled back, a surprised look on his face, and then launched himself at his opponent.

They were on each other, grappling and straining, as each tried to gain dominance. Anthony moved farther back, trying to stay clear of the fight. He couldn't do anything to help, he knew that, but the thought of Freddie getting hurt on his behalf made his chest ache. He felt so helpless.

After a few moments of what seemed like an evenly matched struggle, Freddie reared back and head-butted Brian, hard. As the bald man's eyes glazed over, Freddie wrapped his hand around his throat.

"Go back to New York." Freddie's voice was deep, and the ferocity made Anthony shudder. He wouldn't want to be on the receiving end of that, but damn if it wasn't sexy as hell.

Goatee struggled to speak through his closed airway. His voice was harsh and guttural. "Our master wants him, and our master gets what he wants."

"He's mine." With a growl, Freddie threw Brian against the brick wall to their left. The goateed man let out a grunt as he hit the structure. A cloud of red dust sprang up from the impact. Brian slid down to the ground, looking conscious but dazed. A web of thin, spidery cracks was left behind on the wall above his head.

Just how hard had Freddie thrown the guy? Anthony looked back at him. He hadn't even broken a sweat!

Freddie turned to the other two punks, who had gotten to their feet. One of them hissed, and they both stepped forward.

"What is *wrong* with them?" It was frightening, but also confusing as hell. "Who the hell acts like that?"

Freddie ignored Anthony's question, holding his hand up to the two leather-clad punks, who stopped in their tracks.

"I'm older than you." Freddie's voice had a sense of command in it that made Anthony's blood hum. "By many years."

"Who the fuck cares how old you are?" The two were psyching themselves up for an attack.

"You haven't learned yet what we can do." Freddie made a claw shape with his right hand. Anthony stared, bewildered. What was Freddie doing? Why weren't they attacking? It was as if Freddie had some kind of control over them. Their muscles strained, like a predator launching itself at its future meal, but they couldn't move.

Freddie made a strange flicking gesture with his fingers. There was a strangled cry, and one took off running. The other went for the still-disoriented Brian. He pulled him off the ground and to his feet, although the bald man was unsteady, leaning against the kid.

"Tell your master," Freddie snarled. "Anthony is not for him."

The remaining punk made a low, harsh sound, like a hostile, caged animal, and hoisted Brian over his shoulder. He took off at a clip. Anthony stared as they rounded a corner and disappeared.

Their behavior made no sense. The animalistic sounds, the things they'd said. Anthony was tired of being in the dark about what the hell was going on. These weren't some stalkers or even mafiosos. This was something else. And Freddie knew what it was.

He turned back to Freddie, who winced at the look of fury Anthony gave him.

"What the fuck?"

8

FREDDIE

As they walked back to the hotel, Freddie silenced Anthony with a low grunt of "not here" every time he opened his mouth to ask a question. It wasn't safe to talk in the open. As a bonus, it gave Freddie a few minutes to find an explanation for what Anthony had seen. Although he wracked his brain, he hadn't come up with anything convincing.

Once the door to the hotel room closed, there was no stopping Anthony.

"What just happened?" Anthony stood framed by the doorway, his arms crossed and his face flush with rage and confusion. Freddie didn't like that he'd caused that anger, but it was all to keep Anthony safe. That was what was important.

"They tried to kidnap you. I stopped them." Freddie loosened his tie and sat by the desk. He was acutely aware of the high wire he was balancing on. He needed Anthony to trust him, but he couldn't betray the existence of vampires to a human, even the coven master's nephew.

"Don't play coy with me. They hissed at us. That one *growled* at you."

"They were weirdos."

"And...and goatee guy moved faster. Faster than...well, I don't know, but it wasn't normal." Anthony's confusion warred with his anger, and Freddie wished so badly to lay everything out for him. But he wasn't allowed.

"I didn't notice that." That's the answer Freddie decided on. Weak, but better than the alternative.

"I know what I saw! That was insane. They weren't hired guns."

"The Azarians are crazy." Freddie shrugged. "Always have been."

"That doesn't explain anything. Are they the mob? Are they a cult?"

"...a little of both."

Anthony's face scrunched in anger. He was barely holding it together, and Freddie was helpless to diffuse the situation without saying more than he should.

"No!" Anthony was almost yelling. "Absolutely not. We're not doing that. These people are more than stalkers or deranged fans. What kind of horrible shit is Oliver involved in? Why would they try to kidnap me?"

"Leverage."

"For what? What do they want?"

"I don't know. Business dealings. I'm just security." Freddie cringed inside. He knew it was the right thing, but the deceit made him feel dirty.

"You're just *security*? Come on Freddie, I'm not stupid. You're like some super soldier or something. When you threw the guy with the goatee, fucking Brian, there were cracks in the wall behind him. That's insane!"

"I work out." Freddie chuckled. That Anthony thought of him as a mutant army commando tickled him. And turned him on a little.

"God, you are infuriating!"

Freddie didn't respond. What could he say? Anthony grabbed the hotel phone from the nightstand and put it to his ear.

"What are you doing?" Freddie asked. If Anthony tried to get the police involved, he'd have to stop him. They would make everything a thousand times more complicated.

"I'm ordering room service, dammit." Anthony's voice took on a sickly sweet tone. "*Caro*, send up a burger and fries. Rare. Well, as rare as you'll cook it, then. A double order of garlic fries and a side of mayo."

He hung up and stood by the phone, staring at Freddie. Freddie felt raw and exposed under his glare.

"And what were those things you said? You're older? You had maybe a decade on them, sure, but what did your age have to do with anything?"

"Sometimes, uh, guys like that are intimidated."

"By how *old* you are?!?"

Freddie shrugged. It was warm in the room for some reason. He reached up and took his tie all the way off, unbuttoning his top button. After a moment, he reconsidered and removed his jacket entirely.

Anthony stared at him, and when Freddie didn't respond, he continued, his voice shaking with angry frustration. "Something was weird with them. What aren't you telling me?"

Freddie still said nothing. It's not that he wasn't able to lie, but this was different. There was a burning in his chest, a physical pain at the thought of deceiving Anthony. He'd done that enough. He wouldn't make up some elaborate falsehood. Eventually, Anthony might find out the truth, and for every lie he would hate Freddie more.

"Answer me!" Anthony moved closer to him. "You said that I'm yours. What was that?"

Freddie didn't have a response. He wasn't sure why he'd said that. The Azarian coven master asserting a claim on Anthony had activated a deep rage in him. If Anthony hadn't been standing there, he would have slaughtered the three of them. To hell with avoiding an international inter-coven war.

That disturbed him. Freddie always kept his emotions on a tight leash. Losing control worried him. He couldn't protect Anthony, or his coven, if he was flying off the handle.

"Listen to me," Anthony's voice came out harsh and broken. "I don't have people in my life I can't trust. People that hide things from me. People that take away my ability to make informed decisions. And I certainly don't kiss them. So forget what happened out there. I misjudged you."

The words hit Freddie like a freight train, and as usual, he stood there and took the impact. This was no alley fight, though, and Anthony wasn't some punk vamp. This hurt.

Anthony grabbed his light beige coat from the closet and threw it on.

"Where are you going?"

"Away from you. Don't follow me."

Anthony was out the door and down the hall. Freddie would go after him, of course, but he'd stay hidden. He moved to the window and pushed it open just enough to allow him to squeeze out, pulling it closed behind him.

The brisk, cool breeze coming off the bay cleared Freddie's head. What was his next move? He had stopped Anthony from being kidnapped, but his charge had seen too much. He'd ended up pushing Anthony away, and he didn't know how to get back whatever trust they'd had.

It was dark enough now that Freddie would go unnoticed on the rooftops. Freddie kept his eyes trained on Anthony as he exited the hotel, although it was unnecessary. Anthony's scent was so strong and distinct to him, that delicious citrus and leather, that he could have tracked him blindfolded.

The two kids that the Azarian coven master had sent to kidnap Anthony had been ridiculous. They were 80s stereotypes of punk vamps, and their reactions had been the uncontrolled flailing of the very young. They had to have been turned less than a year ago.

Brian had been older, but still a baby compared to Freddie. As the head of security, Freddie would never have sent new vampires out to capture a hostage. Baby vamps lacked control. They had trouble keeping their emotions in check.

Like he should talk. What the hell had he been thinking, kissing Anthony? No matter what Master Hughes had said, getting involved with someone on a job, with the coven master's *nephew*, was a terrible idea. Anthony had some kind of hold on him, and no good would come of it.

Anthony turned onto a side street. Jumping to the top of a nearby pharmacy, Freddie landed lightly on the tarred, flat roof.

He was out of his depth. He'd always looked down on his coven-mates who pestered Master Hughes about every insignificant problem, but he didn't have a choice. After a moment of deliberation, Freddie reached out with his mind.

Master?

Despite being several hundred years old, Freddie wasn't nearly as powerful as Oliver Hughes, and it was quite the distance from California to England. He waited for the response. Once his master boosted the signal, they could speak normally.

Freddie. I can count on one hand the number of times you have called for me in our long years together. What's wrong?

As Freddie spoke, he kept his eyes trained on Anthony, who had stopped to peer into the window of a bookstore.

We were attacked.

Report.

Three vamps, Azarians. Two very young, the third more experienced. They cornered us in a secluded area. I fought them off. All still alive.

Too bad, but probably for the best. And Anthony?

Physically fine.

And?

Anthony continued down the street, and Freddie followed, leaping across several rooftops. It wasn't a problem to keep up. Anthony was wandering as if he had no clear destination.

He doesn't trust me. The vamps were indiscreet.

What does he think?

Not sure. He knows something was off.

Give me a moment.

Freddie's mind went quiet as his master's consciousness departed. A few more leaps, and he was practically on top of Anthony, who was standing in front of the Whistle Stop, a historic-looking gay bar with 1950s-style signage. Anthony ducked inside as Freddie watched from the roof.

Freddie considered whether to follow him in. He could tuck himself into a dark corner without being seen, but he doubted the vampires he scared off today would be back. Anthony should drink in peace.

Plus, it was a gay bar. The thought of watching Anthony flirt with other men made his stomach burn. Which was ridiculous. Anthony didn't owe him anything. But that didn't tamp down the flames inside.

I spoke with Daniel. He isn't sure how Anthony would react to finding out about you, and about his uncle and me. For a creative, he can be painfully literal-minded.

Freddie didn't answer. An uncomfortable unease bubbled inside of him at the thought of Anthony discovering the truth of who he was. How would Anthony see him? Would he be disgusted?

Freddie?

Yes.

I can tell that something is wrong.

I'm doing my job.

You always are, Freddie. That doesn't mean that you are an automaton.

I'm worried.

About?

He'll see me as a monster.

Master Hughes paused. A wave of his master's compassion washed over Freddie.

Your family was wrong, Freddie. They were wrong about you, and they should have treated you better.

Freddie's chest tightened reflexively. He didn't know what to say. He didn't want to think about his family. The hurt was still too present, too deep, even after centuries. And they hadn't been wrong. He was a monster. He'd done terrible things.

He could never see you as a monster, Freddie, as long as he knows you. The real you. If he trusts you, he'll come around.

He doesn't *trust me.* Freddie felt himself floundering. This was the whole reason Master Hughes had sent him on this assignment, for him to develop his ability to handle people. So far, he was a massive failure.

He will. I know you. You'll do what needs to be done. Freddie didn't answer. Anthony would never come around now.

Regardless, standard operating procedure. Don't tell him about us unless it's impossible to hide, or necessary to save his life.

Yes, sir.

Reach out if you need me.

With that, Master Hughes was gone, and Freddie was alone, crouching in the shadows on the rooftops of San Francisco.

9

ANTHONY

Anthony didn't see Freddie for the rest of the **night,** and after a couple of old fashioneds was doing his best to forget.

The bar was cute, a mix of the historic and the tacky, covered in memorabilia and black and white pictures from the old days. Hollywood icons like Bette Davis and Katherine Hepburn. Burt Reynolds' nude magazine spread. It filled a need that Anthony had to connect with his gay ancestors. He didn't have many blood relations, and sometimes the lack of a sense of history made him feel lost, a lone gay wanderer through an unkind world.

He'd pounded the first drink, but he'd slowed down with the second and surveyed the clientele. There were a couple of cute guys, including a blonde twink with a swimmer's build, wearing a skin-tight beige tank top. He'd glanced at Anthony a few times, and normally, Anthony would be all over it, but tonight was different.

The idea of going home with the guy was unappealing. Which was ridiculous. He was exactly Anthony's type.

The drunker he got, the more he couldn't help thinking about Freddie. Freddie was the polar opposite of Anthony's type. Tall and muscular and strong instead of small and soft. Anthony liked to be the one in charge. Freddie kept trying to impose his rules on Anthony. The bodyguard made him crazy, with his black suits and his perfect face and his broody silence.

That wasn't right. Nothing about him was perfect. Except for maybe the kiss. It had been both tender and incredibly sexy.

If only it didn't come from such an annoying person. Anthony had been a little harsh with Freddie, considering he'd just saved him from being kidnapped. But Freddie knew more about this whole affair. Anthony was tired of being left in the dark.

Anthony finished off the third old fashioned and settled up. Getting tipsy had solved none of his problems, and he had rehearsal the next day. No need to end up even more hungover. He made his way back to the hotel room, swiping his key card and steeling himself for Freddie's presence as he opened the door.

The room was empty. A wave of disappointment ran through Anthony, and he wasn't sure why. At least now he'd have a peaceful night's rest, without the guy sitting in the corner like a sleep paralysis demon.

It wasn't to be. He couldn't get comfortable, and sleep eluded him. Some time around five in the morning, he forced himself out of bed. Still no sign of Freddie.

Not that it should matter. He wasn't speaking to the guy, anyway.

The rest of Anthony's stay in San Francisco was uneventful. Freddie kept his distance, standing at the back of the theater during shows and tailing

Anthony as he made his way through the city. Instead of an intrusive warden, he was now a silent shadow.

Anthony didn't like it.

Così opened to rave reviews, with one reviewer calling Anthony's rendition of his big aria "transcendent." The critics were happy, the subscribers were happy, Rosemary was happy, and Anthony...

Anthony should have been happy. He wasn't.

When he got to the opera house for closing night and climbed the aged wooden stairs to his dressing room, the full weight of his exhaustion hit him. His schedule had always been grueling, but usually the energy of live performance canceled that out. This time, though, he didn't feel energized. He hadn't gotten a good night's sleep in a week, and rehearsals for *Barber of Seville* in Barcelona started in two days.

Anthony opened the door to the dressing room. He hung his jacket on the hook by the door and turned to see a small vase containing three white calla lilies. Small and delicate, they looked as if they were made of porcelain. Next to them on the vanity sat a note written in a beautiful, slanted script.

Anthony –

Your voice blooms on stage like these calla lilies: delicate and perfect. It's an honor to have heard you.

Regards,
Freddie

Anthony stared at the piece of paper in his hands. It wasn't a lengthy missive by any means, but the words seemed honest.

Something settled in Anthony's chest, and a flush of warmth hit his face. Why should he care if the bodyguard liked his singing? The audiences liked it, the critics liked it. He barely knew Freddie. Why did he matter so much?

But the gesture did matter. He had bought the flowers. Written the note. He was more thoughtful than Anthony had given him credit for.

Anthony tried to put Freddie out of his mind for the next two days, with mixed success. He spent most of his time poring over the score to *Il barbiere di Siviglia*. Rossini was his bread and butter, and *Barber of Seville* was Rossini's most popular opera, but Anthony hadn't performed it for almost two years. He needed to refresh himself on the music.

Anthony was waiting to take off for Barcelona, engrossed in the score on his tablet, when he saw movement out of the corner of his eye. Freddie was coming down the aisle, dodging the open doors of overhead bins.

When he reached Anthony, Anthony couldn't help himself. At the sight of Freddie, he could only think of the calla lilies, and of his kind words. He smiled at Freddie. Freddie's mouth went up just the tiniest bit at the corners as he passed.

Butterflies kicked up in Anthony's stomach. Why was he acting like some kind of teenager? Freddie's note had been very sweet, but he was still an enormous pain in the ass. Anthony shook his head, frustrated with how bashful he felt.

The rest of the passengers filed in, and although the flight was almost full, Anthony had an empty seat next to him. He stretched out and settled in, taking his tablet out to study his score. The jet took off, the noise of the engines forming a quiet symphony accompanying the music in his mind.

A little while after they reached altitude, his study was interrupted by a body slipping smoothly into the seat next to him. Anthony didn't need to look up to know that it was Freddie.

Anthony couldn't focus on work with Freddie there. When he couldn't stand it anymore, he broke the silence.

"Thank you for the flowers."

"You're welcome." Freddie's voice was soft and almost...tentative? So unlike him.

Anthony kept his gaze focused on the opera score in his lap, but he was hyper aware of the muscular man sitting next to him. For the first time, Anthony noticed how good Freddie smelled: earthy, with a hint of cinnamon.

He reached over and rested his hand on Freddie's thigh. Hard muscle flexed under the smooth, silky fabric of Freddie's dress pants.

"You don't have to stay in a different room tonight," Anthony said, still not making eye contact. "I know you prefer to be closer. For security reasons."

Freddie let out a quiet sigh.

"Thank you. That would be best."

Freddie placed his hand on top of Anthony's, applying the lightest pressure. It surprised Anthony how smooth Freddie's palm was. He hadn't expected a professional bodyguard to moisturize.

"I...am sorry." Freddie's voice shook as he spoke.

Anthony's brow furrowed in confusion. Was it that Freddie wasn't used to apologizing? Was he worried Anthony wouldn't forgive him?

"It's okay."

"No. I don't want to hide things from you. But...the more you know, the less you'll be able to extricate yourself from all this."

Anthony frowned. That was positively wordy for Freddie, but he wasn't sure what he meant.

"From what?"

"From this...world. My world, Master Hughes' world. It's dangerous, and I want to protect you. I was hired to protect you."

Anthony's stomach dropped with a sudden realization. "What about Uncle Danny? If they're willing to kidnap me for leverage, he must be in even more danger."

"He's with Master Hughes. The safest place in the world is by Oliver's side. He has resources at his disposal. Daniel is untouchable. That's why the Azarians are coming after *you*."

Anthony shook his head. All of this was so murky. "Who *are* they?"

"Anthony, I—"

"I don't care how dangerous it is, Freddie. Daniel is my only family left, outside of my nonna. If he is in trouble, I want to know."

Freddie took in a deep breath and let it out. They sat in silence, but something weighed on his mind.

"The Azarians are a family," Freddie said, bringing his volume down and leaning into Anthony. "They are based in New York."

Anthony found it hard to think with Freddie so close, but he fought through. He needed to understand.

"A mob family?"

"Of a sort."

"I don't understand. If they're in New York, what do they care about what happens in London?"

"Outside of Charles Azarian, the...head of the family, they are all very young. An internal power struggle decimated the ranks about ten years ago. They are rebuilding their influence, and they're branching out."

"All the way across the Atlantic?"

"I've never met Charles Azarian, but my understanding is that his ambition isn't tempered by reason or ethics."

"Seems like a fun guy."

They sat there for a long moment, accompanied by the hum of the engine and the indistinct murmur of conversation. Anthony leaned in and rested his head on Freddie's shoulder.

"Thank you for telling me."

"I..." Freddie seemed at a loss.

"What?"

"I don't enjoy lying to you."

Anthony looked up at Freddie, who was staring straight ahead.

"Okay."

"Or hiding things from you. You deserve better."

Freddie's words sent a warm wave through Anthony's chest. Why did he care about this man's opinion? He'd only known Freddie for two weeks. But here he was, practically snuggled up to him on a flight to Barcelona.

10

FREDDIE

Freddie was the head of security for a vampire coven. Most of his job was hiding their existence and lying to humans. But it was wrong to lie to Anthony. He wasn't sure why, but the certainty of it resounded like a bell deep within him.

"There are things I can't say." He forced the words out. "To keep you safe."

Anthony's hand wrapped around his waist. Freddie had not been this close to another person, human or vamp, in decades. He lived a solitary existence. It kept him alive and sane. He preferred it. Or so he had thought.

"I do feel safe with you."

At Anthony's words, warmth spread throughout Freddie's body, a comforting heat, as if he had just fed. He looked down to see Anthony's face buried in his arm. Anthony was so much smaller than Freddie. It stirred his need to protect. Anthony was a fragile human, but he had a fire in him that deserved to be safeguarded, to be nurtured. Add in the fact that he smelled so damn good, and Freddie was lost.

Anthony's hand ran along the side of his torso, and all thoughts of his job melted away as his cock hardened.

They were at thirty-five thousand feet. Freddie had never cared to join the mile-high club, but Anthony stirred a level of desire in him he thought had faded long ago. He made Freddie feel almost human again.

Freddie looked around. The airplane lights were turned down low and the nearby passengers were mostly asleep. A few wore headphones, listening to a podcast or watching a movie. Freddie leaned down, putting his lips against Anthony's ear.

"With you against me like this," he whispered, letting his deep voice rumble in his chest, "I can't help but imagine how you'd look naked."

Anthony let out a sweet, soft moan. God, playing with him was delightful. Freddie stroked the back of his neck, the motion both energizing him and grounding him.

"Shh, you wouldn't want anyone to hear you. Better stay quiet."

Anthony nodded, keeping his eyes closed and moving his head to Freddie's chest. Freddie flicked his tongue against Anthony's ear, and he squirmed as Freddie tightened his grip around him.

"I imagine you lying naked in front of me, your pretty cock so hard for me."

Anthony managed to keep from moaning this time, but his fast intake of breath sent a jolt of desire down Freddie's spine.

"So hard it hurts. I'm still in my suit, but you're there, totally exposed, waiting for me. When I touch you, you tremble underneath me. I squeeze your cock and it's too much to bear."

Anthony's arms tightened around him, and Freddie growled at the sign of his need.

"I'm so desperate to taste you. I spread you open and run my tongue along the rim of your hole."

Freddie licked down Anthony's neck as Anthony shivered and took in tiny gulps of air. He was trying to mute his reactions, but control was slipping away from him, and it delighted Freddie. Freddie could break him if he wanted to, and god, did he want to. Nothing would be hotter than having Anthony right at the edge.

"I make you suck my finger to get it nice and wet." Freddie tapped his index finger against Anthony's lips, and Anthony opened up. Freddie slipped the digit inside Anthony's warm mouth. Anthony suckled him instinctually. Freddie could tell that his brain had gone offline. Only the desire to please remained.

"Good job, sweet. Then I push into your hole, first one finger, and then two. Once I've got the third in, I'll know you're ready for me."

Anthony let out a quiet sob. Freddie licked a little circle on his neck, and Anthony's breath quickened as he did so. Anthony's skin was delicious, citrus and salt and sweat.

"I unzip my zipper, fully dressed and standing over your naked body, and I take out my cock. It's hard and dripping for you."

Anthony's fingers clawed at Freddie's side, full of desperate desire. Freddie chuckled. Anthony squirmed, hearing it.

"You have to be quiet," Freddie whispered. "When I enter you, you can't make a sound."

Anthony nodded, his eyes still closed.

"I need to know you hear me, baby."

"I…I'll be quiet." Anthony's voice was barely even a whisper.

"Do you promise me?"

"I promise." Anthony's breath hitched, and a tremor shook him. Freddie thrilled at the effect he was having.

Freddie looked down at Anthony, at his angelic face and his pale, bare neck. He was perfect.

"When I push into you, you'll be fuller than you ever have been in your entire life."

Freddie checked the nearby rows one last time. Nobody was looking. He let his fangs drop.

It was dangerous to do this here, where someone might see. And it was dangerous because the demon was straining inside Freddie, wanting more, so much more, clamoring to claim Anthony. But Freddie knew he could never hurt him.

Gently, so gently, he bit into Anthony's neck, barely puncturing the skin, not deep enough to reach a blood vessel. Anthony's whole body spasmed.

Freddie clamped his hand down on Anthony's mouth, preventing his cry from escaping. Anthony trembled, and Freddie held him tight against himself.

The tremors slowed, subsiding into gentle twitches as the orgasm finished. Freddie removed his hand, stroking Anthony's face.

"God, I think I just..." Anthony whispered.

Freddie hummed affirmatively. Anthony's spent form rested against his chest and stomach. He was overwhelmed and floating in the afterglow. Freddie licked his thumb and rubbed it over the bite mark. The saliva would close up the shallow puncture wound, and in a few minutes, it would be nothing more than a fading red spot.

A single drop of blood had been left behind on Freddie's thumb. He couldn't help himself. He sucked it off his own skin.

The flavor of it exploded his senses, growing from an intense tingle on his tongue to a burst of electricity running through his whole body. His vision went white.

What was happening to him? Nothing had ever had that effect before. He'd heard of such a thing once, from a vampire who'd fed from his mate. Could that be what that was? Could Anthony be his?

Freddie squashed the conjecture. He was too old, too hidebound, too violent to have a mate. The universe would never give him such a gift.

"What did you do to me?" Anthony's question came out in a broken whisper, forcing Freddie back into the real world. "That was...I've never felt anything like it."

Freddie couldn't speak. Instead, he stroked Anthony's hair and luxuriated in the sensation of Anthony's body pressed against him.

Eventually, Anthony fell asleep. Freddie sat there, listening to Anthony's slow, even breathing, and already second-guessing himself. Anthony didn't know he was a vampire. He was getting in too deep, and it was with the coven master's nephew. With a human. This was going to hurt.

11

ANTHONY

Anthony **was awoken by a gentle shake.** There was a disorienting moment before he remembered where he was and what had happened. He'd had sex on an airplane. Sort of. At least, he'd had an unexpected orgasm on an airplane. Then he'd fallen asleep on Freddie.

He was afraid to open his eyes. How could this not be awkward as hell? But he didn't have a choice. He couldn't sleep on the plane forever.

Freddie's wide smile greeted Anthony. In the short time they'd known each other, he didn't ever recall Freddie smiling. It made him look even more handsome.

"Hi," Anthony said. "What's happening?"

"We're landing."

"Oh shit. I slept on you for five hours? Shit." Anthony sat up, his face warm with embarrassment. The sleeping part was strangely more vulnerable than the coming in his pants part.

"You were perfect," Freddie said. He brought his fingers up to Anthony's cheek. His touch was soft and gentle.

Anthony smoothed his clothes out with his hands. Freddie didn't seem to regret what happened. Anthony didn't know how to take this version of the silent, hulking bodyguard. He was still gruff, but he had a sweetness about him. It was honestly overwhelming, and a bit terrifying.

There wasn't time to process. Anthony was due in rehearsal that afternoon. He needed to shower, so the two of them grabbed a taxi to the hotel.

The Opera La Rambla was a new house for Anthony, and Barcelona was a new city. As they walked to the opera, Anthony was struck by how beautiful the city was, how romantic. The bright colors and unusual shapes of Gaudí architecture were a surprise that could wait around any corner, and adorable stores and restaurants lined the tourist thoroughfare on which the opera house stood.

In the distance, the spires of the Segrada Familia sprouted up from a sea of single-story buildings, a more than one-hundred-and-thirty-year-old construction project that had just come to a close. Anthony doubted he'd have time to explore this trip, but he made a mental note to leave extra space in the schedule on his next visit.

The opera itself was a beautiful old building, with a facade of white stone and grand windows. The gold-clad embellishments shimmered in the morning sun as Anthony entered to attend his first rehearsal.

The complexities of performing at Opera La Rambla for the first time dulled Anthony's demanding and exuberant nature a bit. Most singers shared common languages they could converse in — Italian, if nothing else — even if they didn't speak the home language of the country where they were performing.

Adrijana Broz, the mezzo-soprano playing Rosina, however, was Croatian, and although her Italian diction was superb, her ability to communicate was limited. She had brought a translator with her, a stout man with wire-rimmed glasses, but he only knew Croatian and English. Many of the opera house staff only spoke Spanish and Catalan.

The schedule was tight, and the language barrier made it worse. It required every ounce of patience Anthony had not to demand that they track down a translator who knew not only Croatian but also English and Spanish.

He didn't dare complain, though. He was already on the defensive. The conductor had it out for him.

"Who's that?" Maestro Alamilla barked at Anthony as he and Freddie walked through the studio door. The Maestro spoke perfect English, with the barest trace of an accent. He did everything perfectly, and he expected the same from those with whom he worked.

"I'm—"

"I know who *you* are, Mr. Bianchi. I hired you. Who's the one in the suit?"

"My bodyguard, Maestro."

"An opera singer with a bodyguard? Ridiculous." The Maestro was a short, elderly man with bushy gray eyebrows that radiated angry authority. Despite his advanced age, he was spry, pacing around the space like a Pac-Man ghost.

"I've had some—"

"He can sit over there." The Maestro gestured to the opposite end of the room. "He had better not speak."

"He'll be quiet—"

"You're late."

Anthony glanced at his phone. It was three minutes before the hour.

"I have a couple—"

The Maestro tapped the gold watch on his wrist. "My room, my time."

Anthony's instinct was to argue back, but this was his first gig at the house and he wanted to work there again. He sulked over to the row of chairs near the piano and sat, fetching his tablet from his shoulder bag.

"You can introduce yourselves to each other later. We're starting with the act two quintet."

Anthony searched through the document for the quintet. He heard the translator whispering to Adrijana, bringing her up to speed. She was barely on her feet when the Maestro raised his baton and gestured to the rehearsal pianist to begin.

The quintet started with each of the five characters entering, and Anthony found it strange to be singing with people whose names he didn't even know. Adrijana had a rising international career similar to his, but the other three were local artists. He had no idea who they were, although he appreciated their enthusiasm. The maestro's rigidity didn't seem to bother them.

About thirty seconds in, the maestro had already stopped them.

"Watch the tempo! All of you are behind. You most of all, Antonio."

"I don't think I was—"

"When I say you're behind, you're behind. From the top, again."

Anthony opened his mouth to argue, but the pianist launched back in.

Over and over, the maestro stopped them, beating his baton on the music stand to keep the rhythm. Anthony had dealt with demanding conductors before, but this was the worst he'd encountered.

After they finally got all the way through the piece, the maestro threw his baton across the room.

It hit the wall with a thud and slid to the floor. His assistant ran over to fetch it.

"That's enough. Antonio, '*Ecco, ridente*' is next. The rest of you are dismissed."

Anthony swallowed as his stomach churned with anxiety. He didn't look forward to tackling his first big aria with Maestro Alamilla. If he wasn't up to snuff, the maestro might throw the baton at *him*.

In the end, nothing got bruised but his ego. The maestro made him sing the first stanza over and over, not allowing him a word edgewise and refusing to move on until Anthony had mastered it to his satisfaction.

A few times, Anthony glanced over to where Freddie sat on the floor, his back against the large dance mirror. He somehow looked suave in the awkward position. Maybe it was all the heat he generated as he stared daggers at the maestro. At a particularly difficult moment, Anthony saw Freddie visibly restrain his impulse to spring to his feet.

Anthony didn't actually want Freddie to beat the conductor up, although the thought of it made him smile.

When he was finally dismissed, Anthony's body sagged with exhaustion. They'd been working for over an hour on one aria, and he was already tired from the trip. He and Freddie walked back to the hotel in silence.

"I could take care of him."

Anthony looked over at Freddie. His face was set like carved granite stone. He wasn't kidding.

"What does that mean?"

Freddie shrugged. "Depends on his response. Some men are more stubborn than others."

"No thank you. I'd like to work here again, and I can't afford bad publicity in the lead-up to Milan. That's the big one."

"Still."

"Your boss wouldn't be mad?"

"He'd understand. I'd explain it."

"Oh. No, I don't think so." They passed an adorable gelato shop. It had a cute little walkup window with carved wooden shutters. Anthony was tempted to stop and get a treat. He'd earned it, after all. But room service waited back at the hotel. He should eat a meal before moving on to dessert.

"Why is Milan so important?"

Freddie's question brought Anthony out of his dreams of ice cream.

"It's difficult to get booked there. It's seen as a stepping stone, a big one. Once you've done well in Milan, all the important international houses start to take notice."

"You're doing well already." Freddie's tone was insistent. "You're busy."

"I am. I want to be less busy."

"What do you mean?"

"I'd rather work less and get paid more. It takes a while before you can negotiate up."

By the time they arrived back at the hotel, Anthony was exhausted and starving. After shoveling down a serving of bland room service chicken tenders and taking off his pants and sweater, he crawled under the covers. Freddie hunkered down in the upholstered chair by the window.

"Uh..." Anthony didn't know exactly what to say. They had done something on the plane, but he wasn't sure what it meant. He tucked the blanket up under his chin with a sheepish smile.

"Hmmm?" Freddy questioned him with a low hum.

"You, uh, don't have to stay in the chair. You could sleep here. With me."

Freddie was quiet for a moment.

"Tempting," Freddie said, smoothing out the wrinkles in his shirt. "But I need to stay alert."

Anthony furrowed his brows in confusion. This had 'lame excuse' written all over it.

"You have to sleep." Anthony pushed, wanting to get a real answer.

"Here and there. But I have to be ready."

Anthony rolled over, curling up into a ball. Had he misread the situation? He thought Freddie was interested in him. He'd been so sweet on the plane, so tender, and sexy as hell. Had Freddie just been toying with Anthony to stop his protests at having a bodyguard?

And what kind of sleep would Freddie get sitting in a chair? At some point, he needed a decent rest. Even if he was some variety of mutant super soldier.

Anthony closed his eyes, willing sleep to take him, but it was a losing battle. His brain wouldn't quiet down, and it was vulnerable sleeping in front of a man he felt...well, something for, even if he wasn't able to define it. He couldn't get comfortable, and the pressure to be ready for the next day made everything worse.

12

FREDDIE

Anthony was upset. Freddie understood why. But joining him in bed would be a mistake. He'd had just a taste of Anthony, and he wouldn't be able to hold himself back. Not again.

His job was protecting Anthony. That was why he was there. Everything else was secondary. He was desperate to have Anthony's skin against his, Anthony's weight wrapped around him, but he wasn't willing to risk letting down his guard.

They were so different. Anthony ran through men like tissues. Freddie hadn't had a lover in decades. Plus, he was a *vampire*. How would he build a relationship with that secret looming over them?

But it was more than just that. It was the monster inside of him. He had done things, unspeakable things, and stood witness to others even more horrible. He would not tie down someone he cared for to a beast.

But that justification didn't temper the confusion and shame radiating off of Anthony. They unsettled Freddie. He only relaxed when he heard Anthony's breath slow to a gentle, consistent rhythm. He hoped the singer would be refreshed when he woke up, and maybe less angry.

The next morning, Anthony didn't speak to him. He readied himself for the day in silence. It hurt, but Freddie took it as a sign that he'd made the right decision. If he was already so thrown by Anthony's frustration, he couldn't allow himself to be sucked in deeper. He had a job to do.

From the corner of the rehearsal room, he watched Anthony continue to butt heads with the conductor, who was intent on tearing Anthony down. It impressed Freddie that he kept his cool — he really must have wanted to make a good impression — but it stoked an unreasonable rage in him. He spent the morning visualizing himself performing various violent acts on Maestro Alamilla.

The afternoon was a staging rehearsal. It was a disaster. Unlike the conductor, the stage director spoke only Spanish, and that meant that the mezzo-soprano, Adrijana, required every direction go through two levels of translation: into English so that her interpreter could understand, and then into Croatian so that she could understand.

Several times, Freddie saw Anthony roll his eyes at how ridiculous the process was, and he didn't disagree. By the time it was over, everyone's nerves were frayed. The rehearsal didn't end so much as it unraveled. At some point, Adrijana left, and someone stood in and took down her staging.

People started drifting out, and Freddie got up to stand by Anthony. Anthony wouldn't look at him.

Anthony was packing up his notes when a woman wearing an apron full of sewing supplies approached. In her thirties, her long, glossy brown hair was pulled back into a ponytail, and she wore heavy black eyeliner.

"*Signor* Bianchi?"

"*Sí, cara?*"

"I'll be your dresser. My name's Gabriela."

"Wonderful!" Anthony grabbed her by the shoulders. "*You* will be my best friend, and we'll survive this travesty together, yes?"

Her eyes darted around skittishly, and she half-nodded.

"Perfect," Anthony said, winking. "Do me a favor and always have a bottle of water on you."

"Uh, of course, *Signor* Bianchi."

"And a handkerchief. I do sweat. Speaking of which, be careful to douse my costumes with the vodka spray after every show. You'd be surprised at how much moisture one man can produce. And dear god, no Febreze. I'm allergic."

At some point, Gabriela stopped talking and was scribbling down extensive notes. When Anthony finished listing his demands, she smiled and scurried away.

The room was now empty, and the silence was back. The lack of communication made his stomach squirm. Freddie couldn't help himself.

"Would you join me?"

Anthony's head snapped to Freddie, suspicion flaring in his eyes.

"For what?"

Freddie saw the hurt underneath Anthony's bitter response, and regret shot through him. He had been the cause. He'd tried so hard to put the job first, but he was also at the mercy of feelings that he hadn't experienced in decades.

"A walk. Then dinner?"

Anthony's shoulders relaxed slightly, but there was still an edge to his voice.

"Okay. Fine."

They left the opera house and strolled in silence for almost twenty minutes, the late afternoon sun casting shadows on the ancient Spanish facades. Freddie had to explain himself, but he didn't know how. His head told him that anything romantic between them would be a mistake, but his body and his soul pulled toward Anthony with an overwhelming force.

Anthony was tired of waiting.

"Did I do something wrong?"

Anthony's question burst through Freddie's bubble of internal rumination. "What?"

"I must have messed up somewhere. I'm not always the easiest. I can be demanding. I don't like rules. But I thought..."

Anthony's voice broke, and a sharp shock of guilt spiked in Freddie's chest. This was his fault.

"No. You didn't."

They continued to walk, the air growing cool as the sun got low enough to hide behind the buildings of Barcelona. Anthony radiated anxiety as he waited for an explanation.

Why wasn't Freddie more of a talker? He'd always been better at doing than saying. He took a deep breath and dove in.

"Master Hughes saved me. I was in rough shape when he found me. He gave me a home and a job."

Anthony glanced over at him. "Rough shape?" Freddie nodded. "I'd been purposeless for a long time. He made me feel useful."

"Oh."

"I can't fail at this job. Master Hughes asked me to protect his nephew—"

"I'm not his nephew," Anthony said, chuckling. "He and Uncle Danny were only just married."

"Step-nephew, then? Family. He needed me to keep his family safe. I could never live with myself if I messed that up."

Anthony slowed to a stop, turning to Freddie.

"We may have just met a few days ago, but you are excellent at your job. Extreme competence recognizes extreme competence."

Freddie smirked at Anthony's positive assessment of his own abilities.

"I don't think you're *able* to get distracted enough to screw up," Anthony continued. "I saw how you took care of those guys in San Francisco."

"They were just punks."

"Still." Anthony tilted his head. "There's something else. What are you afraid of?"

Freddie stared at Anthony. The vulnerability made him uncomfortable, but Anthony needed more.

"I've been alone for a long time. I've never been good at this. And I've done things. Before I met Master Hughes. Violent things. People got hurt. People died. I don't...I wouldn't want you to see me differently. To see me as a monster."

Anthony frowned, shaking his head. "I could never."

"You don't know what I've done. If you did..." Lifetimes of blood flashed before Freddie's mind's eye. Centuries of death.

"Do you regret them?"

"What?"

"The things you've done. Do you regret them? Would you do them again?"

Freddie breathed in, reflecting on his long life. Who he fed on those first few years. The people he killed out of spite or uncontrolled rage. The empty life he had constructed in the ruins of his human one.

When Master Hughes took him in, that was the laying of a new foundation. But still the rot of his old life haunted him.

"I don't regret all. Some things I did to survive, or because I didn't know better. But most, yes."

"Have you tried to make amends?"

By the time he had seen the error of his ways, many of his victim's families were long dead. But he'd done his best to improve the lives of any remaining survivors.

"I have."

"Then what more can anyone ask?"

The answer, of course, was more. So much more. His very existence. But so far he had gone on living, so all he could do was move forward and use his abilities for good.

"I don't know."

"If you've done your best, it's no one's concern. And you sell yourself short in the romance department."

Freddie didn't say anything. His last relationship had been with another vampire forty years before. Damian hadn't been willing to put up with Freddie's work obsession, nor with his silence.

He'd had his own agenda. The whole thing had ended in betrayal.

"I don't know."

Anthony reached up and pressed his palm to Freddie's cheek. "I'm sure of it."

Anthony removed his hand and kept walking. Freddie stood stunned for a moment, then followed a beat later, catching up as they continued without speaking, more comfortable now.

Soon they came upon an enormous park guarded by a whimsical stone structure with a white marshmallow roof. Anthony turned to Freddie.

"Is this where you wanted to go?"

Freddie nodded. "Parc Güell."

"It's incredible."

They walked up the stairs and Freddie stopped at the table to buy tickets. After a glance around the fantastical structures out front, they entered the park.

It was magical. The sun hung low in the sky, painting the greenery with yellow stripes, and enveloping Gaudí's architecture in an amber glow. Anthony grabbed Freddie's hand and kept pulling him eagerly toward the next sculpture. A colorful mosaic lizard climbing a bannister. A huge stone canopy with Roman-inspired columns. Stonework and tile and nature, all of it integrated and interacting in surprising ways.

Warmth bloomed in Freddie's chest when he saw the smile on Anthony's face. He thought over what Anthony had said. It's possible he was right. Being involved with Anthony might not distract him. Perhaps it would fuel him.

Either way, his feelings for Anthony were deepening. He wasn't certain he'd be able to rein them in for much longer.

They reached an empty stretch of path with no statues or art. It was dusk now, and they strolled in quiet solitude. Anthony threaded his arm through Freddie's and leaned against him as they walked. Freddie was filled with a sense of wonder. There was a vulnerability about the way Anthony was with him. It was unlike how Anthony was with anyone else. His trust was a warm blanket, a protection.

He wanted to be that for Anthony.

"I'm sorry I kept my distance," Freddie said, tightening his hold. "But I know myself. I can be protective. Obsessive. If you don't want that..."

Anthony looked away, over the trees and into the sparkling city of Barcelona below. Freddie couldn't tell what he was thinking.

"It's not something I wanted. It's just, when my parents died..."

Anthony swallowed, distress showing on his face. Sadness bloomed in Freddie like a funeral flower. He never wanted to be the cause of Anthony's pain.

"You don't have to tell me," Freddie said. "I understand."

"No." Anthony took in a breath, and tightened his grip on Freddie's arm, although he still looked away. "I want to. My parents died in a car accident when I was seven. They didn't...it wasn't their fault."

Anthony paused, and Freddie leaned down, kissing him on the top of his head. He waited for Anthony to continue.

"It was a drunk driver. The youngest son of some rich family. He'd been out partying, and no one had taken his keys or tried to stop him. He ran a red light, and they were killed instantly. I was safe in the back seat. The kid hit us and sped off."

Tears were rolling down his cheeks now. Freddie was desperate to take this pain away, to eradicate the hurt, but Anthony needed to say this. It was part of who he was, and he was sharing it with Freddie. That was an honor.

Anthony turned back, simmering rage shining in his eyes. "Uncle Danny took me in and raised me. The guy, the man who murdered my parents, got six months of community service. And I...I had a hard time. A couple of years where I was just not good, despite how kind my uncle was, despite the therapy he'd gotten me. But when I came out the other side, I just...I wanted to be in control, you know? I wanted to make the decisions, to captain the ship. To go after my dreams and not let anything stop me. I didn't want that drunk asshole to be the one in charge. I still don't."

Anthony's words hit Freddie like a knife. Physical pain spidered through his nerves and muscles. It was a new, unpleasant sensation. But this moment wasn't about him.

"You deserve to be in charge. I don't want to stand in the way, but—"

Anthony looked up, putting both his hands on Freddie's chest, his eyes still wet with the remnants of tears. "Listen. If you can promise me we will be partners, that we will make decisions together, then I'll concede that you know best about...punching stuff."

Freddie chuckled, his heart opening at Anthony's words. "Punching stuff?"

"I guess you did some wrestling on those steps in San Francisco. Also throwing."

"*Wrestling?*"

Anthony ignored Freddie's faux-outrage. "It's your job, after all. You can be obsessive if you want to be."

Freddie shook his head ruefully. "It's not that I want to be. But if you were in danger…" Freddie's throat closed up at the thought.

Anthony's hands cupped Freddie's face, and the warmth was a balm to his anxiety.

"Hey." Anthony's voice was firm. "I'm not in danger now. I'm here with you."

Freddie looked down at Anthony's open, playful face. There was a vibrancy there that had been absent from Freddie's life for a long time.

Freddie leaned down and kissed him.

Anthony's lips were soft and plump, and a shock of electricity ran down Freddie's spine at the touch. The scent of leather and lemon filled Freddie's nose. He'd never get enough of that. The kiss was gentle for a moment, but Anthony pushed forward and it turned ravenous.

Freddie matched the change, and his tongue tapped at the place where Anthony's lips met. Anthony opened up, and Freddie invaded, tasting and roving as Anthony trembled in his arms. Anthony whimpered, and it spurred Freddie on, his hands moving down to cup Anthony's beautiful round ass.

He fucked Anthony's mouth with his tongue, and Anthony sucked on the welcome intruder as Freddie took control. The blood flowed to Freddie's cock, and he got even harder as Anthony moans grew louder.

After a few moments, Anthony broke it off, breathless. "Damn. You make me want to let you take the lead. You're so strong and...solid. I didn't know I needed that."

Freddie bent down and stole another kiss, tame and sweet this time. "You taste so good."

Anthony reached down and squeezed Freddie's cock through his pants. "I want to know how you taste."

Anthony looked in either direction along the path. It was a more secluded area of the park, and as dusk turned to night, they had seen few other people. Anthony guided Freddie back against a short stone wall and dropped to his knees.

"Anthony—"

"Shh. You don't get to be in control tonight." Anthony undid the button at Freddie's waist and pulled down the band of his navy boxer briefs. Freddie shivered as the cool night air reached his bare cock. Anthony rubbed his cheek against

Freddie's shaft and wrapped his hand around the base.

Freddie throbbed inside Anthony's tight grasp.

"God, you are perfect," Anthony whispered, and then came an intense, wet warmth as Anthony's tongue ran along the underside of Freddie's balls.

"Fuck, you feel so good."

Anthony looked up at Freddie and *winked*, and Freddie knew he was done for. This unreasonable, ridiculous human was never escaping him.

With one swift motion, Anthony swallowed Freddie's heavy girth to the hilt. Freddie thrust forward involuntarily, his cock hitting the back of Anthony's throat.

Anthony didn't gag or move back, instead rocking back and forth a little at a time, as the head slid against the root of Anthony's tongue. It was incredible. He was enveloped inside Anthony's warm mouth.

Anthony hummed, sending electric shocks down the shaft that hit Freddie at his core. He shook at the overwhelming sensations, putting his hands against the wall behind him for support.

Anthony pulled back, his slick lips dragging across Freddie's cock and leaving trails of wet pleasure. Freddie was desperate for Anthony to find a rhythm, but when he did, it was painfully slow. Anthony moved up and down, savoring every taste as his mischievous eyes gazed up at Freddie.

The need was unbearable.

"Anthony, please..."

Anthony quickened, giving Freddie some relief, but it wouldn't last long. Freddie's legs trembled, but Anthony kept up his brutal pace, never going quite fast enough to push him over the edge. A tingling gathered in Freddie's balls, an urgent ache that Anthony refused to alleviate.

"Go faster. Please." Freddie heard the frantic need in his own voice. When was the last time he'd been desperate like this? He couldn't remember. He couldn't remember a time when someone had cared this much about his pleasure. Anthony was hungry for it.

Freddie moaned and bucked as Anthony slowed down the pace even further, then slid off the head of his dick with a pop.

"Do you want to come?" Anthony batted his long eyelashes. Freddie could tell how much he loved to tease. He was in his element.

Freddie nodded, unable to speak.

Anthony flicked his tongue against the underside of Freddie's cock, and it twitched and pulsed in response. He gasped.

Then, without warning, Anthony was off, fast and wet and punishing. Freddie felt his cock hit the back of Anthony's throat over and over, his muscles tightening as he got closer and closer to the point of no return.

When it happened, the intensity was overwhelming. He was gone, his body shaking as he poured himself down Anthony's throat, his eyes clenched tight. He roared, a ragged growl, unable to help himself. It was a feral noise, an animal breaking free from its cage.

The feeling of his fangs dropping dragged Freddie out of the abyss and back into consciousness. He closed his mouth, hiding them. Anthony was still suckling at his cock, squeezing out the dregs of his release.

"That was amazing."

With a last lick, Anthony pulled off and came to his feet.

"It must have been," he said, the words spilling from his swollen lips. "You made sounds I've never heard come out of a man before. They were almost...inhuman."

13

FREDDIE

Careful to keep his fangs covered, Freddie kissed Anthony. It was gentle, the opposite of the animal need he'd just experienced, but the ferocity wasn't gone completely. It stirred within as he tasted his own salty remains on Anthony's lips. When he broke the kiss, he stared deep into his eyes.

"You make it hard to control myself."

Anthony winked at him, his dimples flashing. "I don't want you to control yourself."

"I need to keep you safe. I shouldn't get distracted."

"Is that what I am? A distraction?" Anthony kept his tone playful, but there was an undercurrent of hurt in his voice.

"No. That's the problem."

"I don't see a problem."

"The problem is I—"

Freddie spun around, pinning Anthony between him and the wall as he faced five young vampires. He'd barely heard them approach, his supernatural senses warning him at the last second. They'd been moving fast, faster than any human could see. It was obvious and dangerous. When they came to a stop, a normal person would see five vamps appearing out of thin air. Vampires had spent centuries learning how best to avoid detection, and these idiots would ruin it for the sake of an entrance.

"What the hell?" Freddie heard Anthony behind him. He didn't think that Anthony had gotten a full view of their lightning-fast appearance, but he must have glimpsed something.

The vamps stood in a line facing Freddie and Anthony, and on the right far end was a familiar bald, goateed motherfucker.

"You two should learn to stay in." He smirked with that ugly, punchable face of his.

"Brian? Are fucking kidding me?" Freddie could tell that Anthony was scared, but it didn't stop his incredulous outburst.

"Miss me?" Brian asked.

Freddie was really looking forward to beating the shit out of him.

The five vampires formed a semi-circle around them, each of them decked out in black leather. From their scent, they were only a decade or two older than the ones that attacked in San Francisco. Three of them were gaunt and ragged, like they hadn't fed in weeks. Although Freddie knew that would make them desperate, it might also make them careless.

"The Kiefer Sutherland cosplay is too much," Freddie said, gesturing to their outfits. "Tell Charles that if he wants to have a chance, he has to stop sending babies."

The female vampire in the middle growled. Freddie assumed she was the leader, although that alone indicated how green the group was. Putting your lead in the obvious front position made it easier for an enemy to take them out.

She growled again, showing her fangs. Shit. Freddie would have to explain this to Anthony somehow. That would have to wait, though, since at the moment three of the vamps were lunging for him at once.

Five against one wouldn't normally be a fair fight, but Freddie had a couple hundred years on the lot of them. The more difficult problem was hiding his identity for Anthony's benefit. He had to limit his fighting to human speed, but he should still be able to keep his opponents at bay.

His senses, heightened from experience and age, enabled him to see the hits coming, and he beat back the three vamps without breaking a sweat. Their bones cracked as he landed a well-placed kick and two punches on sternum, hip, and knee. All three staggered backwards, stunned looks on their faces. They had clearly never encountered an older vampire in combat. They'd heal quicker than a human and be fine by morning, but the pain had shocked them.

The leader advanced on him then, her fangs out, her fingers transforming into deadly sharp claws. Her hair, perfectly coiffed in an 80s bob, flowed in the wind as she moved. She was in better shape than the first three. She looked healthy and hale, rather than starving.

Freddie dodged her slash, the tips of her claws passing an inch from his face. He crouched down and rushed her, slamming into her torso and attempting to throw her away from the fight.

She was solid and immoveable. Freddie's impact didn't have any effect, other than to put him in a vulnerable position as she scratched at his back, her knife-like fingernails leaving deep ruts in his flesh. Freddie grunted. The pain was intense, but he had dealt with pain before.

He knew, however, that he wouldn't be able to keep pretending to be human much longer, not if she continued to give him trouble. But he waited, hoping he might avoid letting Anthony see his true nature.

With lightning speed, as fast as he could move and still look credibly human, he circled her, pushing her off her center and ending up behind her. He wrapped his arms around the front of her, pinning her limbs to her sides to limit the range of her claws.

She bit down on his forearm, hard, piercing his skin and muscle through the fabric of his suit. Freddie staggered from the surprise of the injury, but kept himself locked in place.

That's when he glimpsed Brian out of the corner of his eye. He was coming in from the side, moving fast, squeezing past them to get to Anthony. His fangs were out and his eyes flashed with brutality.

He'd reach Anthony before Freddie could stop him if Freddie continued limiting himself to human speed.

For a split second, he froze with indecision, caught between the desire to hide his vampire nature and the need to keep Anthony safe. It was just long enough for Brian to get his hand around Anthony's throat. Anthony whimpered in fear and shock.

With that sound, Freddie was gone.

The red mist appeared in front of his eyes, blurring the world around him, and all noise became a faint echo, as if he were hearing and seeing the world from the bottom of a deep lake. Time lost all meaning as his body moved of its own accord. His impaired senses meant that he couldn't tell what was happening, even as he felt his fangs and claws come into contact with soft flesh. All he knew was the well of rage roiling within him like the caldera of a volcano.

His demon was in charge now. A small part of his brain, kept apart from the overwhelming need to eviscerate, understood that it was his essential vampire nature taking over. He would not be himself again until the demon was sated.

Whether it was seconds or hours later, Freddie couldn't say, but the red seeped away from his vision, and the world came back to him.

On the ground in front of him lay all five vampires, lifeless, their blood pooling around their inert bodies. Closest to him was Brian's headless corpse. He looked down at the object in his hands.

Dead eyes stared up at him from the bald vampire's severed head.

14

ANTHONY

Freddie had gone berserk. Anthony hadn't seen Brian coming, hadn't understood how he'd moved that fast, but his hand had been around Anthony's throat, cutting off his airway. He hadn't been able to force his desperate calls to Freddie past Brian's tight grip. All he'd been able to get out was a pathetic whine.

He had been sure Brian was going to kill him, and he'd thought, silly as it was, that he was glad he'd gotten to give Freddie a blowjob before he died.

But before Brian could tear his throat out, Freddie had exploded.

Anthony missed most of it. Freddie had moved at an impossible speed, a blur in the air as he sprang from attacker to attacker. In the space of a second, they were all down, and Brian's grip fell loose from his throat.

The blur came to an abrupt stop in front of him. Freddie was changed. His eyes shone the red of sunset, and his fingers were long talons. Sharp fangs peeked out from behind his upper lip. Brian's head was in his hands.

"What the fuck just happened?" Anthony stood staring at the carnage.

Freddie looked up at him. Confusion flashed across his face, then fear. He tore his gaze away from Anthony, his eyeballs darting around, looking anywhere else. What was happening? Was Freddie afraid...*of him*?

"Anthony, I..." Freddie's hands went limp and the bald, decapitated head tumbled down to the dirt below.

"What are these people? What are *you*?" Anthony looked around at the carnage, the bile rising in his stomach. Everywhere he looked, blood gushed from deep wounds, and bodies were surrounded by mangled organs and viscera. "You killed them, Freddie. You killed all of them."

Freddie took a step, and Anthony stumbled backwards away from the blood-covered bodyguard. His brain couldn't process what he was seeing. Anthony's chest clenched at the look of anguish on Freddie's face.

"Anthony, you have to..." Freddie's voice trailed off as he shook like he was in the grip of a terrible fever. He collapsed down to his knees.

Anthony's throat tightened at the unusual sight of weakness in the strong, stoic man. His shock and fear evaporated, and he ran forward to Freddie's side, crouching down next to him and steadying him.

"Freddie, what is going on? What do you need?"

"Call your uncle...tell him about *them*...tell him...the crimson surge..." Freddie stopped, unable to say more, and leaned against Anthony for support.

Anthony scrambled to find his phone, pulling it out of his pocket and dialing his uncle.

"Tony?" his uncle asked, his voice scratchy. "It's the middle of the night, what's--"

"We were attacked. They're dead, but the bodies...Freddie can't speak and said something about the crimson surge."

"What? Crimson surge? Are you sure?"

"Yes, I--"

"Anthony." It was the deep voice of Oliver Hughes. "Where are you?"

"Barcelona," Anthony answered. "Parc Güell. Freddie needs help. Please. What's going on? Who are these people?"

"Listen to me. Freddie will be fine in a couple of hours. Get him back to your hotel."

"But--"

"He needs to rest." Oliver's tone was resolute. "I'll send a cleanup crew for the bodies. Your uncle will explain everything in person. We'll take the jet. It shouldn't take us more than three hours."

"What's wrong with Freddie? He's so weak..."

"He'll be okay. Just get him into bed and we'll meet you there. We'll be in the air within twenty minutes."

Oliver hung up the call. Anthony looked down at Freddie, his pale, freckled face marred by exhaustion and pain.

"Freddie?"

Freddie moaned, not opening his eyes.

"Freddie, honey, you have to walk. You can take a nap at the hotel."

Freddie didn't move, his head tight to Anthony's chest. Anthony panicked for a moment. How would he get this man moving? Freddie must have seventy-five pounds on him.

After a moment of consideration, Anthony craned his neck down and touched his lips to Freddie's. It was the softest of kisses, full of a desperate desire for him to be okay. Freddie stirred against him, and his eyes fluttered open, but still he said nothing.

"Come on, Freddie." Anthony squared himself and pushed to give Freddie the support to stand. "I've got you."

It was enough to get Freddie up on his feet, although his steps were unsteady. He leaned against Anthony as they walked, never saying a word. It took some effort. Anthony was half a foot shorter than Freddie, and he hadn't worked out, well, ever. Freddie was pure muscle.

They plodded along the bricks and cobblestones of ancient Barcelona. The light of the moon cast a pale light on the quiet streets, but Anthony took no notice. It was slow going, but seeing Freddie in this state triggered something in Anthony.

No matter what else had happened, Freddie had saved his life. Of that, he was sure. Freddie had put himself in danger for Anthony.

Since the death of his parents, the only person he'd been able to count on was Uncle Daniel. That had stayed true his whole adulthood. If he was honest, he hadn't been willing to let anyone else get close enough. Somehow, Freddie had skirted his defenses.

Freddie had risked his life to protect Anthony. Anthony could support him in the aftermath. Anthony's stomach flipped at the thought. Anxiety, maybe, but something else as well. A jolt of hope. Could they support each other? And more?

Anthony shoved the thought away. He had to get Freddie into bed.

Freddie was out the minute his head hit the pillow. He'd been silent the whole walk back, but as he drifted to sleep, he murmured one word.

"Anthony..."

Anthony's chest tightened with fear. He had to trust that Oliver was right, that Freddie would be okay. But he was alone in the hotel room, sitting and watching over Freddie, just as Freddie had done for him so many nights.

In the quiet, his mind spun with worry. What if Freddie didn't wake up? And what was Freddie? What were those attackers? He hadn't seen much.

The whole fight had been a blur. Freddie's eyes had glowed red. The carnage he'd left behind was...severe. And claws? Had there been claws?

He spent the next few hours focusing on Freddie's breathing. That sound meant that *something* was okay, that Freddie was alive and might come back to him.

He had dozed off in his chair when a loud knock echoed through the room.

Anthony startled awake, his eyes snapping open. He sprang up and looked through the peephole. He was expecting his uncle, but it could be more cult members. Mobsters. Whatever the fuck they were.

On the other side of the door stood Uncle Daniel and Oliver Hughes, both meticulously groomed despite the late hour. Oliver had always dressed in an old-world European style, never without one of his tweed suits. His uncle wore jeans, but they were designer. They fit like a glove.

Anthony opened the door and Daniel rushed him, wrapping him in a tight hug.

"Oh Tony, honey, are you okay? I'm so sorry about all this."

Anthony leaned into the warmth of his uncle's embrace. It was the safe home of his childhood. "I'm okay, Uncle Danny. There were a couple of scary moments, but I'm not hurt."

"I'm so glad, sweetheart."

"I'm worried about Freddie."

"Let me look at him." Oliver's deep voice was a soothing balm. He took Freddie's hand, then bent over him and *sniffed*. What the hell was he doing?

Anthony held his breath. Freddie had to be okay.

Oliver let Freddie's hand drop down to the mattress. "He'll be fine by morning. This is normal."

With those words, something broke in Anthony.

"Normal?" Anthony asked, trembling with rage and fear. "Nothing about any of this is normal! Who are those people? *Were*, I should say, because they're all dead, every last one of them. Are they people at all? Is Freddie? What is Freddie? Hell, what are you?!?"

"He's a vampire, sweetie." Daniel's hand came to rest on Anthony's shoulder. "So were the people who attacked."

Anthony recoiled, suddenly light-headed. He took a deep breath. "A fucking vampire? Are you serious?"

"He is," Oliver said. "Freddie is a vampire. As am I."

Anthony spun around to face his uncle. "You married a *vampire*?"

A small smile teased on Daniel's face. "You can accept the existence of vampires, but it's the fact that I married one that's weird?"

"I don't have much of a choice, do I?" Anthony collapsed down into the nearby armchair. "I saw the fight. Or rather, didn't see it, since everyone was moving so goddamn fast. There had to be some kind of supernatural explanation. I thought Freddie was some kind of government experiment, a mutant super soldier or something. I didn't think it would be vampires! And I don't understand why you'd marry one."

"Because I fell in love." Daniel opened and closed his mouth, like he wanted to say more. Finally, he spoke. "I'm a vampire as well."

"You are not! You're my uncle." Anthony's hands clamped to the arms of the chair. He had to find some kind of solid mooring.

"I am. But I'm also a vampire. Ollie turned me on our wedding night."

"Ollie?!" Of all the insane things Anthony was learning tonight, the fact that anyone would call someone with as commanding a presence as Oliver

Hughes by the nickname "Ollie" was the most discomfiting.

"Don't repeat that." Oliver's voice carried both humor and menace. "Danny's the only one that can call me that."

"I'm sure you have questions, Anthony." Daniel patted Anthony's shoulder. "I know this is a lot."

"It is. I do. Did it hurt becoming a vampire?" The words flew out of Anthony's mouth unbidden. Why did he want to know that?

"It did. It was a rough couple of days. But now I can be with Oliver for hundreds of years, instead of a few decades."

"Wow." Anthony kept glancing at Freddie as they spoke. He looked so peaceful now that he was resting. Beautiful, his face a pristine porcelain sculpture. He forced his gaze back to Daniel.

"Do you drink blood?"

"We do. Never from the unwilling. And usually not in the donor's presence. Oliver and I drink from blood bags for sustenance. The act of drinking can be a very sensual one, and once a vampire finds their mate, they don't want to share that experience with anyone else. But the makeup of vampire blood and human blood is dissimilar, and each provides different nutrients."

"Mate?"

"Yes, Oliver is my mate. Fate intended for us to be together. When a vampire meets their mate, the beast inside of them, the demon, as some vampires call it, can sense the connection, even if the conscious mind hasn't figured it out yet. When mates find one another, it is a special and sacred event."

Anthony shook his head. This was a whole new world. Vampires were a new species. It was overwhelming.

"That's...that's incredible."

"It is." Oliver's voice rumbled from across the room. "Finding Daniel was a defining moment of my life."

"Same, lover." Daniel winked at Oliver.

"Sunlight?" Anthony asked, breaking their annoying banter. "I've been outside with Freddie during the day multiple times."

"It's fine," Daniel answered. "Younger vampires are weaker in the sun, sometimes lethargic, but the older a vampire gets, the less they are affected."

"Garlic?"

"Are you kidding me?" Daniel chuckled, his eyes lighting up. "Like I'm going to stop eating Nonna's lasagna."

"Do you have to be invited in to enter someone's house?"

"No. Although vampires do tend to be unfailingly polite. A side effect of trying to stay hidden in the human world."

"Can you turn into a bat?"

"God, I wish!"

"How...how can you die?"

Daniel lost his smile, his face taking on a serious cast. "It's not easy, but it's possible. A stake to the heart, or decapitation. Sometimes, these old vampires forget that they're not invincible. You have to watch out for that with Freddie."

Anthony just nodded, not entirely sure what Daniel meant.

"I need to get back, sweet," Oliver said. "I have to convene a war council to decide what to do about the Azarians."

Oliver walked over and put his arm around Daniel's shoulders, the suit material straining around his muscles. "Do you want to stay with Anthony?"

"Do you want me to stay?" The worry shone on Daniel's face. "I can."

"Do you think they'll attack again?" Anthony asked.

Oliver shook his head. "No. They'll be licking their wounds for a bit. Regardless, I've stationed a couple of my people downstairs, just in case. You will be safe until we can figure out our next move."

"I should be okay, assuming Freddie wakes up in the morning like you said." Anthony glanced over at the bed. Freddie's face was peaceful, but fear still sputtered deep inside Anthony. What if he didn't? What if he had given up everything for Anthony?

"He'll be out for a few more hours, but then he'll be as good as new." Oliver smiled with pride. "He is the best of my coven."

"What caused the...whatever he called it...the crimson surge?"

Daniel and Oliver glanced at each other uneasily. Daniel turned back to Anthony, compassion in his eyes.

"That's not our place to say, honey. Freddie needs to tell you for himself."

15

FREDDIE

Freddie drifted in a cocoon of warmth. Not a heavy sleeper when he was human, as a vampire he'd snap awake after an hour or two. This slow, cozy return to consciousness was an unfamiliar experience. He was at peace, and he didn't want to open his eyes.

He slowly became aware that the heat was not only from blankets piled on top of him, but also from the warm weight of an arm around his waist. The soft rise and fall of gentle breath tickled his neck.

Freddie's eyes snapped open to assess the situation. Anthony was next to him in the bed, his face angelic in sleep, his cheek resting on Freddie's chest. Feeling Anthony against him made his heart catch.

But would Anthony want to stay by his side once he understood? Freddie stared at the out-dated white ceiling tile, his thoughts racing. What had Anthony seen during the fight? Everything after was a vague fog.

Somehow, Anthony had gotten him back to the hotel. Freddie was wearing only his boxer briefs. Had Anthony undressed him? His clothing must have been soaked with blood.

Anthony deserved better. If he was the reason for the crimson surge, Freddie still wouldn't force Anthony to be with him. He didn't have any idea about Freddie's world. He should be with someone who wasn't a killer.

"I can feel you thinking. Stop it."

Freddie turned his head and kissed Anthony on the bridge of his nose. Anthony scrunched his face up reflexively in response. He was adorable.

"Hi sweet."

"I'm so glad you're awake." Anthony's arm tightened around Freddie's waist, testing and confirming the solidity of Freddie's presence. "Oliver promised me you would wake up, but I was worried."

Freddie pulled away to look into Anthony's eyes. "You spoke to Master Hughes?"

"After the fight, you were so weak, and you couldn't speak. I didn't know what to do. Oliver and Uncle Danny came here."

Fear lingered on Anthony's face like a shadow. Freddie brought his hand up to Anthony's soft cheek, stroking it.

"I'm sorry you went through that."

"You were only protecting me." Anthony smirked. "And *someone* needed to tell me what the hell was going on, because you weren't going to."

Freddie flinched. "Tell you what was going on?"

"You know, that you're a vampire and all that."

Freddie hoisted himself up onto his elbow, keeping his eyes trained on Anthony.

"What did they say?" His stomach flipped with anxiety. He trusted that Master Hughes had his best interests at heart, but he didn't want Anthony to feel pressured.

"Pretty much everything, I think, except—"

"You don't have to be with me, Anthony. There's nothing forcing you. I would never take your choice away. You deserve better than the life you'll have with me. I'm a vampire. I kill people. I try not to, but I do what I have to do. You should find someone who can be your partner and supporter. Someone human."

Hurt and confusion flashed across Anthony's face, and eyes welled with tears. "I don't understand. Are you breaking up with me? We weren't even really dating, I know, but I thought...I thought there was more."

"There is, sweet. But you have the right to choose. You shouldn't be saddled with me."

"I...I don't...we're not getting married. Why does it feel like you're calling off our wedding? I was hoping you'd be my boyfriend, but if you don't want that..." The tears slid down Anthony's cheeks. "I get it. I'm just a job to you. I'm so embarrassed."

The sight was a knife in Freddie's chest. He reached out and grabbed Anthony's arm, and Anthony pulled away.

"No, oh no, my love, I never want to be the cause of your tears. What *exactly* did Master Hughes tell you about vampires? Did he explain what happened during the fight?"

Anthony shook his head, sniffing. "Uncle Daniel said that you should tell me about...about the crimson surge. Whatever that is."

Freddie clenched his free fist. Damn it all, he had assumed they'd told Anthony everything. He'd made a mess of things, and worse, he'd made Anthony cry. He vowed to never do that again.

"Do you want me to go?" Anthony asked. "I can leave you to rest."

Freddie hated the fear and sadness in Anthony's voice. Anthony moved to get up, and Freddie grabbed his hand.

"Please, Anthony, let me explain. Will you?"

Anthony stared at him, and Freddie squeezed his hand, trying to project everything he felt for him through the physical connection. Anthony nodded, sitting and leaning back against the gray satin headboard. But his shoulders were still tense, his body on guard, as if he were waiting for another blow. Freddie had to make this better.

"What happened during that fight was not normal, not even for a vampire. It was what we call the crimson surge. It's a sort of mindless, instinctual rage, where the vampire essence, the demon, takes over and bypasses all human thought. It turns us into a killing machine. It's never happened to me before." Confusion flashed across Anthony's face. "It hasn't? Why...what made it happen?"

"Only two things can trigger the crimson surge. When a vampire is in mortal danger. Or when someone threatens their mate."

"I knew you were outnumbered," Anthony said, "but I guess I didn't realize you were in so much danger."

Freddie just had to say it. "I wasn't. You were."

Anthony's eyes went wide. Freddie continued.

"When Brian had his claw around your throat, I lost my mind. My vampire essence, my demon, took over. I would never slaughter my adversaries like that, not when I could subdue them easily enough. But the minute you were in danger, my control was gone."

"I'm your mate?" Anthony's voice was soft and tentative, the polar opposite of his normal boisterousness. Freddie wanted to hold him, to wrap him up and never let him out of his sight.

"Yes."

"Oh."

"But that doesn't mean you're stuck with me. What you want matters. I would never force you to be with me because of some sort of ridiculous vampiric predestination. I would never want you to hate me because you didn't have a choice."

Anthony cocked his head, his expression unreadable.

"Why would I hate you?"

Freddie sighed, rubbing his eyes with his hand.

"Because you don't know what I've done."

"I know you, though." Anthony's tone was strong and insistent. "You have kept me safe. You've put my life before your own. I don't care what you've done."

"You should." Freddie sprang up from the bed. He wobbled on his feet, a little residual weakness from the fight still affecting him. But he had to push through.

"Freddie, I—"

"No." Freddie held up his hand to Anthony. "Just let me get this out. Then you can choose for yourself. I've...I've never told anyone the full story, not even Master Hughes. But you should hear it."

Anthony nodded, concern lining his face. Framed by the headboard, Anthony was like an old painting. The moonlight illuminated his olive skin, and his dark hair contrasted with the gray fabric behind him. He was beautiful. And distant, untouchable.

Freddie pressed on. Anthony deserved to hear it all.

"My sire was not a good man. He was selfish, a petty lordling with a desire for more power and an insatiable need to cause others pain. He turned me because...well, I'm not entirely sure, although I have some ideas. My name back then, over two centuries ago, was Frederick Grosvenor."

Freddie paced around the hotel room as he spoke, needing an outlet for the nervous energy bubbling inside of him. He stared down at the pattern his feet made on the burgundy carpet.

"The Grosvenor family today has no reason to know me, a second son who disappeared in a murderous rage in the 1700s. But back then, my family was important. Wealthy, yes, but we also had political power. And Henry Calvert wanted it."

Freddie stopped and stared out the window. He didn't want to see Anthony's face as he told his story. To see the fear and disgust. He wasn't sure he'd survive that.

"He ambushed me in a London alley on a moonless night. Took me by surprise. Then he turned me. When I awoke, I was in my own bed. My family had sent out a servant to find me. The man had piled my unconscious body onto a wagon and brought me back to the estate. I woke up before they could track down a doctor."

Freddie gripped the windowsill, his fingernails making indents in the old white paint.

"When you first become a vampire, Anthony, the hunger for blood is all-consuming. Usually, the bond shared between a vampire and their sire controls that ravenousness. The sire can calm the demon through that bond and prevent the vampire from rampaging. Henry left me alone on the street. Perhaps he thought I would cause a public bloodbath and discredit my family. Perhaps he simply didn't care, thinking to use his control over me to advance his own political interests."

"The person sitting by my bedside when I woke was my younger sister, Daphne." Freddie's old grief sprang up as the image of her sprang to his mind. He fought through. "She was...she was beautiful. Sixteen, with rosy cheeks and a constant smile. She was who I loved most in all the world."

Anthony coughed and shifted on the bed. Freddie couldn't bring himself to look over at his mate. He kept his eyes trained on the gibbous moon hanging low over the tiled roofs of Barcelona. It was like a searchlight shining down on him, exposing him, leaving him nowhere to hide.

"I was out of my mind with hunger. I barely remember it, the sound of her screams and the blood running down my chin. When I regained my senses, all I had left was despair. And rage."

Freddie closed his eyes, and his mind conjured the memory of his sister's body, lifeless and cold. It hurt, but he deserved the pain.

"My father found me in that state. He reacted...well, how else could he react? There was no room for sympathy or understanding, and rightly so. I stood over the corpse of his only daughter, covered in her blood. He called me out for the monster I am. I left before he could get his hands on a weapon."

Freddie shunted the memory of that night away into the recesses of his mind. He couldn't dwell on that if he hoped to get through this.

"I slaughtered Henry Calvert and his entire family. I wish I could say it was my newfound desire for blood, but no. I did it for revenge. For making me into a beast. For my sister's life."

"After that, I disappeared. I couldn't face my mother and father again. Daphne, she...she was so kind. So innocent. And I murdered her."

"I don't know why I didn't kill myself. I might have thrown myself into the fire, or asked another vampire to behead me. But I didn't. I kept going, at first trying to drown my memories in blood and debauchery. But as the years passed, I needed a purpose for being. I had to balance the evil I'd done. I was searching for ways to do that when Master Hughes found me."

Freddie stopped. There was nothing left to tell. Now Anthony had heard what he'd done, the bloodthirsty brute he was. He still couldn't force himself to face his mate. The rejection that waited there would break him. It might finally be the thing that ended him.

"So you see why I am unfit to be anyone's mate, nevermind someone as perfect as—"

"Freddie." Anthony's tone was certain, insistent. "Freddie, look at me."

It took an intense effort, but Freddie turned his gaze back to the bed where Anthony sat. Anthony's face was red. He'd been crying. Oh god, had he hurt him that deeply? Freddie had thought he would be angry, disgusted, afraid. But this was worse.

"What happens to you if I choose not to be your mate?"

Freddie swallowed. He hadn't expected that question, although he should have. It was one he'd hoped that Anthony wouldn't ask, but he also wouldn't lie. Not to his mate. There would no longer be any deception between them.

"I will never be with anyone else. A mated vampire has no interest in another. And someday, when you die, as humans do, I will also die."

"You'll lose your immortality?"

"Yes. Now that I've found you, our lifespans are tied together, and if you do not become a vampire, I will share your death."

Anthony sat there, taking in Freddie's words, his hands clasped tightly in front of him. The silence was oppressive. Despite his supernatural strength, he thought he might collapse under the weight of it, and under the weight of Anthony's gaze.

Anthony stared at him, chewing his lip and processing everything he had said. Then something in Anthony shifted. He set his jaw and reached out his hand.

"Freddie, I...I'm so sorry for what you've been through." Anthony's voice caught in his throat. "It's more than one person should have to bear."

Freddie blinked in confusion. What was Anthony saying? His mate's eyes were bright, the moonlight from the window reflecting off of them, giving him an otherworldly presence.

"Please don't keep yourself from me," Anthony pleaded. "Come back to bed."

Freddie's mind was a maelstrom of confusion and hope. He managed to get his legs to move, and he crossed the room and laid down next to Anthony. He was careful not to touch him, though. The fear of rejection was too strong.

"Did you do evil things?" Anthony's voice was low and comforting. "Yes. But evil was done to you, enough to break anyone's spirit. You have made yourself who you are today, someone who is honorable and good, someone who protects others. That is an astonishing feat."

Freddie tasted salt as his own tears hit his lips. Had he cried once in the hundreds of years since he became a vampire? He didn't think so, not since the day his sister died.

"You shouldn't be with a killer like me." The words were glass in Freddie's throat, but he had to say them. He had to give Anthony the chance. "You deserve better."

Anthony rested his hand on Freddie's chest, and Freddie trembled at the touch. He was a vampire with inhuman strength, yet Anthony could reduce him to a quivering mess. Even this tentative, careful caress made him weak.

Then, without warning, his lips were on Freddie's, ravenous, as if he was trying to press his very life into him.

Freddie broke the kiss, surprised by the intensity. "Anthony?"

"I don't want you to die. More than that. I want to be with you. No one makes me feel the way you do. Cherished. Seen. I don't know if this whole mate thing is real, if this is forever, but I know how I feel right now."

"Promise me you'll be honest with me." Freddie wanted more than anything to luxuriate in his love's affirmation, but he forced the words out anyway. "Promise that if you are unhappy, that you won't stay and be miserable. I never want that for you. I never want you to be stuck mated to a monster."

Anthony's hand moved to the back of Freddie's neck, his grip strong, pulling Freddie's face in close to his own. His eyes shone with a possessiveness Freddie had never seen in him before.

"If you are a monster, you're *my* monster. You belong to me."

16

ANTHONY

Anthony had taken in so much new information in the previous twenty-four hours that his brain was at capacity. He didn't want to learn more about vampires and the hidden world he'd been thrust into. All he wanted was the sexy-as-fuck man he was currently kissing.

His tongue pushed into Freddie's mouth, licking, flicking against the tip of Freddie's own. He was ravenous, searching and sucking as if Freddie was a flask of water and Anthony hadn't had a sip in weeks. Freddie moaned, and Anthony's tongue vibrated and tingled with the sound. Freddie's noises were like the sweet melody of an oboe in a Bach sonata.

Reluctantly, he separated himself. Freddie smiled at him, so open and vulnerable, and Anthony knew that Freddie's smiles were only for him. Freddie didn't give them away to anyone. Only Anthony had earned them. A warmth spread in his chest at the thought.

Then Freddie's smile turned into a blistering smirk, and Anthony's cock filled as his desire built. God, this man was everything.

Anthony ran a hand down Freddie's bare torso. "Are you feeling better?"

"I'm fully recovered."

"You know, I didn't know you could speak for more than a sentence at a time. You just talked for like ten minutes straight." Anthony grinned.

Freddie pushed him away jokingly. "Don't get used to it."

Anthony sprang into action without a thought, straddling the muscular vampire with one quick motion. Freddie's eyes twinkled at Anthony's eagerness. And Anthony was eager. He wanted more than the furtive moments they'd shared before tonight.

"It's okay. I don't need words."

He kissed Freddie once more, but he soon left those soft lips behind and licked and nibbled his way down Freddie's square jaw to his long neck. As Anthony's tongue flicked against the pale skin of his Adam's apple, Freddie's moan rumbled in his chest. Anthony was hard then, harder than he'd ever been in his life. Freddie's thick length pushed against Anthony's thigh as it strained against his boxer briefs.

As he continued his way down, Anthony ground his ass against Freddie, rubbing Freddie's hardness between his cheeks. Anthony had to have Freddie inside of him. He almost never bottomed. It had always been too vulnerable, but now his need was unbearable. He craved that vulnerability.

He nibbled at Freddie's nipple, which pebbled as his teeth grazed it. His eyes burned with lust as he gazed up at his red-haired lover.

"Please, I..."

Freddie ran his hand through Anthony's thick hair. "What is it, my sweet?"

"Will you take control? Will you take *me*?

Freddie laughed, deep and strong, and Anthony's balls tightened. Dammit, he would not come without this man inside of him.

The room spun for a moment, and Anthony found himself on his back. Freddie lay on top of him.

"Is that the vampire strength and speed I've heard so much about?" Anthony asked, wiggling a little underneath Freddie to relieve his painfully hard erection.

"It is." Freddie winked, and in a blur, Anthony's underwear was gone. Freed from the only thing holding it back, Anthony's dick sprang to attention, pre-cum dripping from its slit.

"What a pretty cock my mate has."

Then Freddie's hand was around his balls, massaging them with his palm. Freddie trailed soft, feathery kisses up his thigh. Anthony squirmed, and Freddie held Anthony's pelvis in place with a strong grip.

"You're not going anywhere," Freddie said, the fire in his eyes warning Anthony that the muscular vampire was the one in control. Anthony shuddered.

Freddie licked a stripe up the underside of Anthony's cock, and Anthony's whole body jumped. He thought he was losing his mind, he was so desperate.

"Please. Please suck me. Freddie..."

Anthony yelped as Freddie took him in, the head of Anthony's penis hitting the back of Freddie's throat. The sensation was incredible, wet and warm. Freddie moved his lips up and down the shaft. Anthony drifted, closing his eyes and floating in the cloud of ecstasy.

As Freddie went faster, though, the telltale tightness built in his balls.

"No, I don't want to come." Anthony whined. "I need you inside me."

Freddie chuckled, Anthony's cock still in his throat, and Anthony shook as he attempted to maintain control. Freddie sucked hard and removed his lips with a *pop*.

Without warning, Freddie pushed Anthony's legs back against his chest, and his tongue found its target: Anthony's hole.

"Oh fuck!" Anthony couldn't control the noises he made as Freddie invaded him. It was so much all at once. Lightning shot down his spine, fire ran along his skin. No one had ever rimmed him before. The sensation was like nothing else.

Looking down, all Anthony could see was the shock of Freddie's red hair as he consumed him. Freddie savored him, licking and nibbling relentlessly, flicking his tongue and then pushing in deeper. Anthony squeezed his eyes shut, holding onto the back of his knees, instinctively pushing against Freddie, pulling him in further.

Anthony whined when the sensation disappeared, but that was soon replaced with the stretch of Freddie's finger, slick with lube, exploring him. He opened his eyes to see the hunger on Freddie's face, intense but also wicked and playful.

"You're so tight." Freddie licked his lips. "How long has it been?"

"Years. Not since college. I don't...I don't normally bottom."

"Good. This sweet treasure is just for me."

Freddie slipped a second finger in and slowly moved it in and out of Anthony. There was a slight burn, but that was soon gone. He leaked pre-cum onto his stomach as Freddie fucked his fingers into him. It was overwhelming, but so, so good.

"No more. I need you," Anthony begged.

"Sweet, I don't want to hurt you."

"You won't. Please." Anthony pulled his legs further back against his chest, desperate for Freddie's cock inside of him. He knew Freddie was large, but he also knew that if Freddie didn't fill him soon, he was going to explode.

"Tell me if it's too much."

Anthony gasped as Freddie removed his fingers. Then came intense pressure as the tip of Freddie's cock pushed into him, stretching him out. God, Freddie was thick. Anthony didn't mind the burn. It proved that he was alive.

Freddie was moving too damn slow. "I can take it, Freddie. Push."

And with that, the vampire was inside of him. There was a sharp pang, but it soon faded to a dull throb. He was full, so full. Damn, he had needed this.

As Freddie leaned forward and kissed him, Anthony wrapped his legs around Freddie's waist, making sure that he was as deep as he could be.

"You feel incredible, my sweet."

Anthony stared into Freddie's eyes, desperation and hunger taking him over. "Move. You have to move. Fuck me."

Freddie began, slow at first, careful and tender. Anthony's need was too great. His hands traveled down Freddie's back to his ass, grabbing onto the thick muscle and encouraging Freddie to speed up.

"Harder, Freddie," Anthony said. "You can't break me."

Freddie's eyes flashed, and he was off, building to a punishing rate. It was everything Anthony wanted. They could be tender later. For now, he wanted Freddie to own him, to prove that Anthony was his.

He couldn't control the moans escaping from his lips, animalistic and raw. Over and over, Freddie filled him, stretching him and proving his desire and lust. He knew he was what Freddie wanted, all that Freddie wanted.

Freddie shuddered, and from the look on his face, he was close.

"Come inside me, Freddie. I need it."

Freddie's eyes flashed, and his fangs dropped, sharp and shining. In a flash, Anthony understood.

"Do it," Anthony commanded.

Freddie roared as his orgasm hit and locked his teeth onto Anthony's neck. There was a quick pain, and Anthony came harder than he ever had in his life, spraying all over their stomachs. He shook, and as Freddie drank, he gasped. It was as if his orgasm never ended. With every mouthful of blood, Anthony trembled, crying into Freddie's chest, tears running down his face even as pleasure racked his body.

He felt Freddie disengage, licking gently around the tiny wound. Exhaustion hit Anthony in a wave, and his eyes closed against his will.

"Sleep, my perfect Anthony." Freddie's voice purred in his ear. "Sleep, my prince."

Anthony let go, drifting off, wrapped in contentment and warmth.

17

FREDDIE

When Anthony's phone rang for the third time, Freddie woke him up. He'd hoped to let him sleep late - it was his day off, and he deserved the rest after the night they'd had - but Freddie worried it was some kind of emergency. It was after noon, and they had some important things to talk about, anyway.

He reached down to jostle him awake, but stopped himself as he took in Anthony's sleeping form. He sprawled out like a starfish. His limbs had claimed the bed the minute that Freddie had left, as if he was a king and the hotel mattress was his domain. His chest rose and fell, and his face was so peaceful that Freddie regretted interrupting his slumber.

"Sweetheart?" Freddie shook Anthony's shoulder.

"Hmmm?" Anthony stretched but didn't open his eyes. "Do you want to have sex again?"

Freddie chuckled and kissed Anthony on the forehead. "Always, my sweet, but your phone's been ringing off the hook for a couple of hours now."

Anthony's eyes popped open. "Weird. No one has my number. My nonna, my agent, Uncle Daniel, a couple of friends, that's it."

Freddie tossed Anthony the phone. He glanced down.

"My agent. It's before seven in New York. What could be wrong?"

Anthony sat up, scrunching his toes as he woke himself up fully. He hit a button and held the phone to his ear. Freddie settled down into the armchair and smiled. He never expected to have moments like this. Domestic. Ordinary. Just him and his mate dealing with life like normal people do.

"Josh, what's going on?" Anthony said into the phone.

As his agent spoke, Anthony blinked in surprise. Freddie tried to distract himself. With his supernatural hearing, he could make out what the person on the other end was saying, but it was rude to listen in without their knowledge.

"I...of course, the answer is yes. There's a two-week window between Barcelona and Milan. I should be able to squeeze those dates in. Will I rehearse with the rest of the cast?"

Anthony chewed his bottom lip. He was practically vibrating with nervous energy.

"Okay, that will have to be enough. Have them send me a video so I can learn the staging. Get back to me with the contract info when it's finalized."

Anthony tossed the phone down on the bed, a look of shock on his face.

"Anthony? What's going on?"

"They want me to jump into a role at the Manhattan Lyric. They lost their Tonio for *La fille du régiment* because of a family emergency, and the general manager doesn't think the cover is ready."

Anthony rocked back and forth on the cream bedspread.

"This is the big one, Freddie. It's the most important opera house in the country, and the role is a tour de force. If it goes well, I'll start having more control of the parts I take. If it's a *triumph*, it could change the course of my career. I..."

Freddie got up and sat next to Anthony, putting his arm around his mate's shoulders, soaking up his warmth as he squeezed Anthony to himself.

"You are a star," Freddie whispered.

"You don't have to say that."

"I don't have to, but it's true. I've seen your talent and your dedication. Everyone else will, too."

Anthony nuzzled into Freddie's chest, feeling Freddie's strong pecs through the thin fabric of his undershirt.

"Thank you for believing in me."

Freddie kissed the top of his head. "Always."

They sat there for a long moment. Sex was one thing, but this was something different, something neither had experienced before. A lover who was also family, who would support them and perhaps build a life with them. Freddie felt incredibly lucky. And incredibly anxious.

"But it complicates things," Freddie said, wincing as he did.

Anthony pulled away a little from Freddie, his brow furrowed in confusion. "What?"

"Master Hughes will not like it. I'm sure he already wanted to increase your security detail. Not that it's necessary. The death of five vampires is a blow to any coven. Normally, that would be enough for them to leave you alone. There are other ways to get at the coven master."

Anthony cocked his head. "But?"

"New York is Azarian territory." Freddie's jaw clenched. "If you go there, they won't be able to resist an attempt."

"I wish I understood better what all of this is about."

"I only know what I've told you," Freddie said. "I've kept nothing from you, and I won't from now on."

Freddie's phone beeped from on top of the desk. He disengaged from his mate, walked over, and picked it up, glancing down at his notifications. He grimaced.

"Master Hughes has met with his war council. He wants to talk to us."

"Okay?" Anthony looked up at Freddie, shaking his head in confusion.

Freddie looked his lover up and down. Fine hair covered his olive skin, culminating in an absolutely delicious-looking treasure trail. His nipples were the perfect size, and Freddie loved how responsive Anthony was when he played with them.

However, now was not the time to be thinking these thoughts.

"You, um, probably want to put on a shirt."

Anthony's eyes widened, and he sprang into action, running into the bathroom to make himself presentable. Freddie plugged his laptop into the hotel television and sat on the edge of the bed. Anthony had just sat down next to him when Master Hughes appeared on the computer screen.

The coven master looked regal in a gray vest with a deep purple shirt, his deep blue eyes twinkling with humor. Anthony's uncle was at his side in an oversized plaid sweater. He was bouncing with excitement.

"I'm pleased to see you both awake and safe." Freddie's master winked at him. "I assume you've told Anthony everything?"

"Yes, Master Hughes," Freddie answered.

"Good."

"It's really wonderful, Anthony!" Daniel leaned in front of his husband, his face filling the screen, so close to the camera that only his nose and mouth were visible. "Having a vampire mate has so many benefits. I'm happy for you."

"I...thank you, Uncle Daniel. It's a lot to take in."

"Let me know if you want vampire sex tips. Or if you ever need to vent about you-know-who."

"He's sitting right there, darling." Master Hughes pulled Daniel back away from the camera with a look of adoration. Master Hughes never smiled like he did when he was with his husband.

"I know he is!" Daniel said. "That's why I was talking in code," he said in a stage whisper.

Freddie's face warmed as he blushed. It was a rare occurrence, and was only possible because he'd fed from Anthony.

"Can we deal with the issue at hand?" Freddie said, covering up his sheepishness with an all-business tone.

"You can do some stuff with your hands," Daniel said, "but that's not my favorite."

"Uncle Danny!" Now Anthony was beet red.

"Yes, darling, let's get back on track." Master Hughes put his arm around his husband.

Daniel pouted for a second, then kissed Master Hughes on the cheek. "Fine."

"You have done an excellent job at protecting Anthony," Master Hughes began, "but the Azarians are throwing more fire power at him than we expected. I have a strong relationship with the largest Italian covens. Freddie will be sufficient for your next few days in Barcelona, but when you fly to Milan, a larger vampire detail will be waiting for you."

Anthony turned to Freddie, questioning. Freddie nodded. Even if it complicated things or made him angry, Master Hughes had to know.

"I'm going to New York," Anthony said.

"What?" Daniel's voice was strained. "You can't do that!"

"Darling." Master Hughes patted Daniel's hand, then addressed Anthony in a soft but commanding voice. "Your uncle is right. New York is the one place you have to avoid. Charles Azarian wouldn't hesitate to throw every available vamp he has left at you."

"What is his problem, anyway?" Anthony asked, his vehement tone betraying his anger and frustration. "Why is he coming after me? Why does he want to get at you two?"

Master Hughes sighed. "There is no ruler of the vampires, no king. Every coven is independent. If there *were* a leader, however, it would be me. I have managed, through some degree of skill and an even greater degree of luck, to negotiate a peace among the most powerful covens across the globe, with only a couple exceptions. The Azarian coven is the most powerful of those exceptions."

Master Hughes' eyes hardened, and Daniel rested a hand on his forearm.

"Charles rejects any check on his power. About a decade ago, he took out the bulk of his relatives in a bloodbath the likes of which we haven't seen in centuries. He rallied the young ones to his side with promises of power and influence, and the freedom to hunt and kill as they liked. He sees me as the linchpin holding together the current peace, and he wants to use you as a bargaining chip to break that peace. Chaos and violence would be preferable to him, and allow him to expand his own rule."

Freddie's whole body tensed. He hadn't known how eager Charles Azarian was to take out his master. It made him want to fly to New York alone and kill Charles himself.

"That's not all." Daniel's tone was deadly.

"No." There was a hint of something that Freddie had never heard in Master Hughes' voice. Was it shame?

"Charles was a lover of mine for many years," Freddie's master continued. "I thought he understood. We weren't mates. There could be nothing more than friendly affection between us. But somehow he convinced himself that I was indeed his mate. I broke it off years ago, but...for him, this is not only political, it is personal. He still thinks I belong to him. Because of that, I believe he will not stop, even if it decimates his coven."

Freddie's stomach burned as if he'd swallowed hot lava. His mate would be in danger until Charles Azarian was dead. His blood hummed with resolve. No one would take his Anthony from him.

"He was my friend, once." There was a deep sadness lingering in Master Hughes' eyes.

"It's too dangerous to go to New York." Daniel said, the metal in his voice showing his resolve. "You can't put yourself that close to him and his people. He's unhinged."

Freddie turned to Anthony. He was lost in thought, and Freddie couldn't read his expression. After a long silence, Anthony spoke.

"I'm going."

"Tony--"

"No, Uncle Danny. This is the biggest moment of my career so far. If I let this pass by, I may never get the chance again. I refuse to let some vampire madman stand in the way of my moment. I'm going."

Master Hughes frowned, and his voice rang in Freddie's head. *You have to convince him.*

"Don't speak into my mind." The harsh, insubordinate words flowed from his lips, and he could not stop them, as if he were an outside observer to his own body. He had never gone against his master, not in the decades he'd served, but he couldn't stop himself. "Anthony is right here. He has a right to hear anything that is said about him. If my mate wishes to go, then he will go, and I will be there by his side to protect him."

Master Hughes' face grew dark. "He is human, and fragile."

"Don't talk about me like I'm not here," Anthony said, his voice like ice. "This is my life we're talking about. I make the rules. I'm going to New York."

Freddie put his arm around Anthony's shoulders. He would give his own life if it meant helping his mate achieve his dreams.

"Tony, I don't like this." Daniel's face was white with fear. "You shouldn't put yourself in danger. What if--"

"What if I had died here, in Barcelona? What if? There are no safe places. I'm going."

"That is our decision." Freddie's words held a note of finality. They were mates now, and they would stand together.

The four sat there in silence, two in Barcelona and two in London, the air filled with tension and sadness and icy determination. Finally, Master Hughes spoke.

"I don't condone this, Freddie, but I can't fault you for siding with your mate." Master Hughes had a look of resignation on his face. "I'll help however I can."

"Ollie--"

"Their minds are made up, love." Master Hughes ran the back of his hand over his mate's cheek, calming him, and then turned back to the camera.

"There will be a contingent of three vampires waiting for you in New York. More than that will attract attention." Master Hughes' eyes pierced into Freddie. "Do well by them. They will be putting themselves in danger, entering hostile territory with you."

"Of course, coven master." Freddie let out a shaky breath. He knew he had made the right decision, but that didn't mean there wasn't danger. What would they find waiting for them in New York?

"Tony..." Daniel was on the verge of tears.

"This is the biggest opportunity I've ever had, Uncle Danny. It could change my life."

Daniel didn't speak for a long moment, nodding as a watery smile appeared on his face.

"I love you."

"I love you, too," Anthony replied. "Everything will be okay."

18

ANTHONY

Maestro Alamilla continued to be an **enormous pain in the ass,** but in the wake of what Anthony had survived, he couldn't seem to stay angry at the man. He felt sorry for his co-star Adrijana. The language barrier had exacerbated the conductor's martinet attitude, and he was constantly correcting and belittling her. Anthony made a point of giving her encouraging smiles whenever they sang together. She seemed grateful, and her perseverance in the face of all the criticism was impressive.

Three major events enabled Anthony to let the Maestro's abuse roll off shoulders. His upcoming debut in New York. His deepening affection for Freddie. And his newfound friendship with his dresser, Gabriela.

She was an absolute delight. Thank God she spoke English so well. That meant she could gossip, and she was great at it. He'd had a costume fitting after a particularly frustrating rehearsal with the Maestro, and she'd validated his complaints about him.

"*Gilipollas!*" she shouted. "He was always bad, but ever since his chorus boy fiancé broke up with him last year, he's been a monster."

"Oh, do tell." This was the kind of thing Anthony loved.

Gabriela bent to help the costume designer tie up Anthony's boots. They were made of worn leather and had a surprisingly high heel. "Everyone says Rafael left because the Maestro couldn't...um, what's the English? Get it up?"

Anthony giggled. The costume designer Ignacio, a fey, elderly Spaniard in a pinstripe suit, shot Gabriela a murderous look, but she just rolled her eyes.

"He doesn't have any English," she whispered, tilting her head toward the old man, "so don't worry. He can't understand you."

"How old is Rafael? Maestro Alamilla must be sixty-five."

"Rafael got the job right after university. The Maestro was a guest instructor there. And he isn't sixty-five. He is seventy-five."

"Holy shit!" The costume designer slipped a white fabric belt around his waist, closing the burnished silver buckle. "To each their own, but that's quite the age gap."

"It was a tremendous scandal among the choristers." Gabriela winked and smiled. Anthony loved how much she loved drama.

"I'd imagine."

Ignacio stepped back from Anthony, gesturing dismissively. Anthony checked himself out in the mirror.

"You're dashing." Gabriela squinted, reaching out to the back of his neck. "But do you think maybe the collar..."

"It needs to be tighter, yes!" Anthony grinned. He was finally working with someone who knew an inkling about style. "And the jacket wants a brighter lining." He glanced at Ignacio, who looked on, stone-faced. "Will you tell him?"

"Of course."

Gabriela and Ignacio proceeded to have a heated argument in Spanish. Although Anthony understood little of it, Gabriela was a tiger. The old man didn't stand a chance. Eventually, he threw up his hands and walked away, one end of his measuring tape trailing behind him.

"Is everything okay?" Anthony asked.

"He's mad, but he'll do what I say. Everyone does."

"Ooh, I like you." Anthony smiled, then squinted at Gabriela. "Never use that on me."

In the days leading up to opening, Gabriela and Anthony became inseparable. She was good at her job, methodical and calm, as well as being an inveterate gossip. With Gabriela and Freddie by his side, Anthony was unfazed by the Maestro's criticism. In fact, he was more confident than he ever had been. Opening night came soon enough, and when the curtain rose on the first scene, a thrill of excitement rushed through Anthony unlike anything he'd experienced since his early days as a young artist. Opera La Rambla was full, hundreds of eager faces surrounded by lush velvet and gold-plated furnishings.

Freddie sat in the front row, dapper as all hell in a tailored black tuxedo, towering over the little old ladies on either side of him.

This was new. Anthony had someone there who supported him, who loved his art and his talent not because he was a rising star, but because Freddie loved *him*, warts and all.

Was that right? Did Freddie love him? This whole mate thing was confusing. On the one hand, it was like something out of an old romantic movie, as if an army of violins could come on at any time to underscore the big moments of their relationship. On the other hand, did Freddie even get a choice? Would he have wanted to be with Anthony without it? Anthony hoped so, but he wasn't sure.

He thought Freddie loved him. He knew Freddie would always protect him, that he would always be there for him. Did he love Freddie?

He felt *something*, something that he'd never experienced before. A longing and a need, but without the desperate heaviness of youthful infatuation. This was light and buoyant. Anthony didn't worry about Freddie's devotion waning. He knew it wouldn't.

He took a deep breath, grounding himself, and sang.

"Piano, pianissimo, senza parlar, tutti con me venite qua."

He tried not to look out at his mate, but he couldn't help himself. At the sound of his voice, Freddie's eyes sprang to life with adoration. Happy tingles spread through Anthony's stomach. With some effort, he wrenched his gaze away from Freddie's perfect face. He had an opera to sing!

The performance flew by in a whirlwind of music and applause. Despite his assholery, the Maestro was an excellent conductor, and Anthony felt the company and the orchestra fall into sync, breathing as one and spinning out gorgeous sound. The ovation at the curtain call lasted for ten minutes, and Freddie was the first to his feet.

After changing clothes and squeezing in a quick makeout session in his dressing room, Anthony walked into the opening night party with Freddie on his arm. Everyone's eyes went to them.

"They're all looking," Freddie whispered in Anthony's ear. "You're a big star. You shouldn't be with a bodyguard. You should date someone impressive."

Anthony turned to his vampire, seeing an uncharacteristic self-consciousness on Freddie's face. He kissed him on the cheek.

"They're staring because we're sexy as hell," Anthony whispered. "And you're not a bodyguard. You're the head of security for Hughes International. You *are* impressive."

Freddie didn't seem convinced. Anthony squeezed his arm and led him into the fray. Several of the elderly donors rushed over to Anthony, gushing over his performance. Most of them gave Freddie a once over and ignored him, but Anthony made a point to introduce him to everyone. Freddie looked uncomfortable, but Anthony understood that this was a bandage they had to rip off. Dating Anthony meant having to play trophy husband on occasion.

Of course, Anthony knew Freddie wasn't the sparkling conversation type, but that was okay. Anthony could do that. He appreciated Freddie's broody silence. He didn't need to say more, he just needed to find his confidence.

After a few exchanges, Freddie settled in. Once he understood all he had to do was play the heavy, he took to it eagerly. After a few minutes of boring small talk with some elderly millionaire, Freddie would glare, and then the person would make an excuse and leave. It was an excellent system.

An older woman in a black Chanel suit approached them, speaking in accented but grammatically perfect English. Gold rings covered her fingers, and her silver hair was perfectly coiffed.

"Antonio, what a triumph!" She spoke a little too loud, as if she were performing for the whole room. "You and Adrijana were brilliant. I suppose it was nice to have a hometown Figaro as well. I pray we can lure you back here next season."

"Thank you for that, Señora..."

"Martí. Nuria Martí. I'm the president of the board for Opera La Rambla. And the company's largest donor." The woman winked at Anthony. There was something predatory about it that made Anthony uneasy.

"I'm also a high-ranking senator in the Cortes Generales," she continued. "My connections in the government enable much of what happens here at the opera."

"That's incredible." Anthony glanced at Freddie, whose face was inscrutable. "This is my partner, Frederick. He works in security."

"Ah, yes, the bodyguard I've heard about." Señora Martí leaned in, talking in a stage whisper.

"You should find someone more suitable for your career, *querida*."

Anthony blinked in confusion. One thing he'd learned from working in different countries was that sometimes folks were more direct than appropriate when speaking a language other than their own. He hoped she was just being accidentally tactless.

"I—"

"It's no fun, but relationships aren't just about romance. Who you date is a business decision, sweetheart."

"Listen, Señora Martí." Freddie's voice was a rough growl. "Anthony—"

"You are very tall, which is nice. But Anthony is smarter and savvier than you. He has a bright future ahead, and you will only hold him back." The older woman plastered on a disingenuous smile. "Take it from someone who can make or break his career."

Freddie didn't reply, clearly flummoxed. Anthony was confused. Why was she threatening him? Was it that important for her to throw around her influence? Why would she care who he dated?

An aggressive female voice speaking rapidly in Spanish broke the tense silence. It was Gabriela, and from all appearances, she was ripping Nuria Martí a new asshole. She stood in a stunning black gown, bedecked in sequins, with her hands on her hips. Señora Martí had a dazed look on her face at the unexpected assault.

When Gabriela stopped speaking, Señora Martí's eyes were searching for the exit. With a sharp movement of her head, Gabriela indicated that the older woman should speak to Anthony and Freddie.

The board president took a deep breath. "My apologies. Gabriela has informed me I have spoken out of turn. I did not intend to offend."

"Uh, it's okay—"

Gabriela cut Anthony off. "I'm sure Señora Martí has many duties to attend to right now, considering the importance of her position."

The older woman nodded and rushed away, making a beeline for the powder room.

"Thank you, *cara*," Anthony said. "I didn't know how to handle that. Will she give you trouble?"

"Not a chance," Gabriela answered. "I've dealt with her before. She's always been that way. She thinks she knows what's best for everyone, even strangers, and she likes to throw her political weight around."

"I'm not sure why she would care."

"She doesn't, not really. It's part of her evening's entertainment. Luckily, she's a bit of a coward, and she knows she can't do anything to me."

Anthony was about to make another comment when he realized Freddie hadn't said a word. He turned to his handsome mate.

"Freddie?"

"She's right. You are smarter than me. I'm not good with people."

"That's just not true. You're smart, and you're good with the people that matter. You're good with me."

Freddie shook his head. "You deserve better."

"The hell I do." Anthony looked up at Freddie, taking his face in his hands. "You are what I want. I can be shallow enough for the both of us. Who cares what some wealthy fossil says?"

Freddie didn't say anything. His jaw clenched and his lips pressed together tightly. Anthony did his best to project how much he cared for Freddie through his eyes.

"You are the one that's important to me," Anthony said. "Don't doubt yourself."

"He's right, *querida*." Gabriela's smooth voice broke the intimacy of the moment, but Anthony didn't mind. "The more famous Antonio gets, the more people will monopolize his time. Don't change who you are. Having a scary bodyguard boyfriend is an advantage."

Freddie looked at Gabriela, then shrugged. Maybe hearing that from someone other than Anthony had broken through his self-judgment a little. "I guess."

"I promise you it is true."

"You are fantastic!" Anthony said. Gabriela was a master of these petty social games. "What are you doing after we close? You should come to New York with me."

"They expect me here to work on *La Sonnambula*. God, I hate that one."

"Whatever they're paying you, I'll beat it. All the big stars travel with their personal dresser, but I've never found anyone that I clicked with. You're perfect."

Gabriela thought for a moment and flashed a wide smile.

"I would love to."

19

FREDDIE

The remaining time in Barcelona was **quiet,** with no hint of a threat from the Azarian coven. Freddie distracted himself from his growing unease about the trip to New York by taking Anthony on every romantic excursion he could think of. They visited the Sagrada Familia, the Picasso Museum, the gothic quarter, and stepped foot in every Gaudí building in the city.

And the food! So much *paella*. So much gelato. So much *jamón*. Although Freddie didn't need to eat, and didn't beyond a few bites here and there, he adored feeding his mate. The look of ecstasy on Anthony's face when he bit into the perfect *croqueta* was maybe the sexiest thing Freddie had ever seen.

The time together brought out a different side of Anthony. Freddie loved Anthony's mischievous bent and his hot temper, but the sweet moments they shared were a wonderful surprise. Soon enough, though, they would have to enter the lion's den. They couldn't escape it.

Anthony, Freddie, and Gabriela sat together on the trip back to the US. Anthony and Gabriela chatted like old friends the entire flight, as Freddie calmed his anxiety by sorting through their security measures.

Three of Freddie's team from the London coven would be waiting at the terminal for them. Freddie's plan was to play the visible heavy, and ask his coven-mates to stay hidden. There would be no sightseeing in New York. They would either be at the hotel or at the opera house, and Freddie would be by Anthony's side the whole time.

The plane was entering its descent as Freddie pushed away his obsessive rumination. He found Anthony and Gabriela engaged in a heated, whispered game of "what animal are the other passengers?"

"He's a giraffe, no question," Anthony's voice was deadly serious. "Look at that neck. And that huge ass tongue. Why does he keep licking his lips like that?"

"A giraffe?" Gabriela's face was incredulous. "His nose is so skinny and long. I agree on the tongue, though. He's an anteater."

"An anteater! What do you know about anteaters? They don't even live on your continent!"

"You think we don't have books? Besides, I went to university in Mexico, and got my master's in Texas."

"Texas!" Anthony clutched at imaginary pearls.

"Why do you think I speak English so well?"

"You have a grad degree? In what?"

"Futurism."

"What the hell is that?"

"It's the science of predicting the future."

"Why are you working as a dresser?"

"I didn't want to get a P.h.D. to teach, and there aren't a lot of other jobs in the field."

"Who could have predicted that?" Anthony asked in a sarcastic tone.

Freddie chuckled, and both Gabriela and Anthony turned their heads towards him. Anthony leaned over and kissed him on the cheek. "Welcome back to the land of the living."

"What do you mean?"

"You were lost so deep in your thoughts that you didn't answer the flight attendant when he asked if you wanted pretzels."

Freddie furrowed his brows. "Oh."

"It's okay." Anthony grinned. "Now that you're awake, do you think that dude over there is a giraffe or an anteater?"

Thankfully, at that moment, the front wheels of the plane touched down, ending the conversation with a bump and a screech.

Freddie recognized the three vampires in black suits waiting for them at the baggage claim. Two of them, Rose and Lillian, were twin sisters, both of them tall and Black with dark brown hair. Rose wore her hair short, almost to the scalp, while Lillian kept her's down, straightened, often in a ponytail. Freddie knew them to be smart and insightful. They'd led several complicated investigations for the coven, and Freddie trusted them to keep Anthony out of danger.

The third was Garrett. It wasn't often that Freddie questioned his coven master's judgment, but Garrett? He was a killing machine waiting to be pointed at a target. Anyone who had ever called

Freddie quiet should meet Garrett. He avoided speaking. He was loyal to the coven, but still. Garrett wouldn't give a shit about protecting anyone once he got into a rage. His only purpose in a fight was carnage.

Freddie feared few people alive, vampire, human, or otherwise, but he'd hesitate before going head-to-head with Garrett. Short, tan, bearded, and built like a spark plug, the man excluded an aura of strangeness. He had seen no evidence, but the rumor in the coven was that Garrett had been turned not as a human but as some other paranormal species. Perhaps a werewolf, or even a redcap.

When they reached the three, none of them said anything. At first, Freddie was confused, until he realized they were all staring at Gabriela. Freddie nudged Anthony, who immediately figured out the problem.

"Uh, Gabriela, will you go on to the hotel?" Anthony asked. "These are some, uh, business associates of Freddie that we need to meet with."

There was a flash of something on Gabriela's face, perhaps anger at being dismissed, but it was quickly gone.

"Of course," she said. She nodded to the group and headed off toward the busy taxi stand.

The vampires stood in silence as Gabriela walked away, her burgundy carry-on rolling by her side. Anthony rolled his eyes, but Freddie knew it was prudent. Once she was out of earshot, Rose skipped the introductions and dove right in.

"Any developments?"

"No. We'll proceed as expected to the Hotel Burton Midtown." Freddie clocked the frustration on Anthony's face. "Anthony, this is Rose and her sister Lillian from the coven. That is Garrett."

Rose and Lillian nodded. Garrett did not.

"Rose and Lillian, the two of you should plan on staying hidden." Freddie was all business. "Report back anything suspicious."

"And if we see one of the Azarians?" Lillian asked.

"Take them out. We're not taking any chances. Try to stay quiet, if possible. And no going rogue, Garrett."

Garrett let out an annoyed grunt.

Rose gave him a sharp look. "We'll keep an eye on him. There's a black car out front. We'll follow you to the hotel."

"I can't have all of you hanging around during rehearsal," Anthony said. "And I'll have Gabriela with me most of the time. She's my dresser and my friend, I won't send her away."

Anthony was already annoyed at the situation. Freddie had hoped this would go smoother.

Lillian led the vampires off, speaking without looking back. "We'll stay out of the way. You won't see us again unless the worst happens."

As Anthony watched the group walk away, Freddie removed their luggage from the carousel.

"The all-black looks are a lot," Anthony commented. "Do members of your coven always dress like some weird mix of CIA agents and mafiosos?"

"Master Hughes likes the uniformity of it."

"Unless you're hiding in the shadows, a gang of people in black suits sticks out."

"Vampires don't need clothing to camouflage themselves."

"All the more reason to add a dash of color." Freddie chuckled, stacking the luggage and wheeling it towards the exit.

"I'll pass along the feedback."

The Hotel Burton was lovely, if nothing spectacular. The room was spacious, with simple but luxurious furnishings in gray and chrome. The bathroom floor was heated, which made Anthony happy.

They were in bed within the hour, with Anthony's head tucked into Freddie's armpit. The feeling of rightness suffused Freddie as he lay there. Neither of them were in the mood for more than sleeping, with Anthony on edge about stepping into a major role in two days, and Freddie worried about keeping him safe. But despite the uncertainty, Freddie felt a deep satisfaction that Anthony trusted him with his life. Anthony might not be a vampire, or even fully believe in the idea of mates, but Freddie's body coursed with the need to protect his beloved.

Although Freddie didn't sleep, having Anthony snoring into his side was the most restful sensation he'd ever experienced. When the sun peeked through the hotel's sheer curtains, he jostled Anthony awake.

They arrived at the Manhattan Lyric at ten in the morning, standing for a long moment outside to take in the huge, elegant opera house. It was overwhelming, built in the 1920s in the Beaux-Arts style, with arched windows, balustrades, bas-relief panels, and sculptures of figures from Greek myths. It exuded a bluster of enforced permanence. While the Opera La Rambla projected a cozy antiquity, this building was yelling out "I exist!" to the entire world.

Freddie heard a hitch in his mate's breath as they surveyed the landmark. He reached out and grabbed Anthony's hand, intertwining their fingers.

"It's just so much, you know?" There was a scratchiness to Anthony's voice. "I've always dreamt of being here. Part of me thought it would never happen. "

"You're here because of your talent and hard work. You deserve it."

Freddie turned to Anthony as a tear trailed down his cheek. Freddie wiped it away.

"Never doubt it, my love," Freddie whispered.

Anthony smiled, his eyes bright. Freddie kissed the track on Anthony's cheek, tasting the sweet saltiness. "Let's go inside so you can be a star."

Anthony giggled and nodded.

It was good they took the moment outside, because once they arrived at the rehearsal studio, there was no stopping. Anthony had weeks of rehearsal to catch up on. The assistant director for the production, Tara, was a no-nonsense woman sporting a long mohawk she'd put up into a braid. She ran Anthony through his blocking with brutal efficiency. Freddie sat in a corner of the large, rectangular room, sending Anthony little bursts of silent support any time he seemed confused or overwhelmed.

In the afternoon, the conductor came in and hit the big musical ideas. He was a bearded, chubby man with a rosy complexion, and he was an extraordinary pianist. The polar opposite of Maestro Alamilla, he covered all the important moments while still encouraging Anthony to explore.

To Freddie, Anthony seemed more in his element, although it was obvious there would never be enough time. Anthony needed to trust his own instincts. Freddie was certain that if he did, he would give an incredible performance.

At the end of the rehearsal, a short bespectacled man in his sixties with a bland featureless face entered the room, crossing to Anthony and shaking his hand.

"Good to have you, young man." His voice was a tad too nasal to be pleasant.

Freddie watched as Anthony's shoulders tensed. "Happy to be here, Mr. Fitzpatrick."

"Call me Henry. I may be the general manager of the most important opera house in the world, but I'm not *that* conceited."

From the smug look on his face and the gold Patek Philippe watch around his wrist, Freddie surmised he was, in fact, that conceited.

"Okay...Henry."

"Who is that?" The little man shook his head dismissively at Freddie.

"That's my bodyguard."

"Aren't you a bit early in your career to be needing security?"

"Uh, yes, well, I've had some issues..."

"He cannot be backstage during the performance."

"Oh, I—"

"We've had the most famous singers in the world tread the boards here, Antonio, and any entourage has always watched from the audience. You'll have a few seats reserved in the front row, house right."

"Um, I guess—"

"There won't be any problem with this, will there, Mr. Bianchi?"

Anthony swallowed. "No. Of course not."

Freddie clenched his jaw, biting his lip to prevent him from saying anything. His instincts screamed that he needed to stay as close as possible, that they couldn't risk being separated, but he didn't want to jeopardize Anthony's big break.

"Your dresser is waiting in the costume department with the designer. You'll get a quick fitting, and she can go over your changes."

Anthony nodded slowly, looking down at the floor. Freddie could tell he was feeling overwhelmed.

"Wonderful. Glad to have you on board."

Mr. Fitzpatrick strode out of the rehearsal room like a towering monarch, despite his short stature. Freddie found himself irritated. No one got to manipulate and control Anthony, not even the general manager of the Manhattan Lyric.

"I don't like this." The words were out before Freddie could stop them.

"It will be fine." Anthony smiled, but Freddie knew that it hid the fear and anxiety that he himself was feeling.

"Maybe you can talk to him again, try to convince him—"

"You heard him, Freddie, his mind is made up." Anthony shoved his score into his shoulder bag with too much force, straining the canvas. "This is just how it is."

Freddie wracked his brain, running through potential attack scenarios. "I could hide up on the catwalk."

"That would be better than being in the audience? You'd be the same distance away. Maybe farther."

Freddie paced around the now-empty rehearsal room, full of uncharacteristic nervous energy and needing a place to put it.

"The backstage is enormous. I'd blend into the shadows. No one would realize."

Anthony shook his head. "You don't think Mr. Fitzpatrick won't notice that your seat is vacant, after he specifically forbade me from having you backstage? And again, how far away will you need to be to stay hidden? There are plenty of areas where the first row is closer than where you'd be."

"There has to be a solution that keeps you safe." Anthony closed his eyes, sighing, and pulled his chin to his chest, stretching his neck. "I don't see it, Freddie. You'll just have to be in the audience."

Freddie came to an abrupt stop by the black upright piano. This was not acceptable. His purpose was to protect Anthony. If he couldn't do that, he had no purpose at all.

"This isn't worth it. It's not safe."

Anthony's face went blank. "This is the most important job of my career so far."

"You'll be in danger."

"I'll be fine."

"No." Freddie began to pace again, caught in his roiling worry. "If I can't be by your side to protect you, you can't do it."

Anthony's eyes flashed, and he clenched and unclenched his fists.

"You think because you've had your dick in me you can dictate what I do? Just because you declare that I'm some sort of magical boyfriend for you, I have to follow your rules? Fuck that. This is my life. I make the decisions. You're either okay with that or you can get out."

Freddie froze. He knew he was treading on thin ice, but every drop of his vampire blood cried out to safeguard his mate. His demon was screaming.

"Anthony, please—"

"No." He turned his back to Freddie, starting out the door. "I have a fitting. Either come along and support me, or leave. I honestly don't care."

20

ANTHONY

Anthony knew he had hurt Freddie, but there was no space in his brain for relationship drama. His mind was overflowing with notes and melodic phrasing and staging and the overwhelming pressure of his upcoming debut.

Gabriela was waiting for him in the costume department. Together, they sorted through each of his outfits to make adjustments and plan out the backstage changes. Freddie trailed behind, silent and brooding. Anthony ignored the mix of frustration and anxiety stirring in his gut.

What if Freddie was right? Maybe he was putting himself in danger by going on. But Freddie couldn't keep him wrapped in bubble wrap. This was the most important day of his career so far! He wouldn't allow anyone to sabotage it.

This was why he didn't date. It wasn't possible to combine his life with someone else's. Opera was his passion, and he wouldn't back down from that for some boyfriend, even if said boyfriend was handsome and caring and annoyingly protective...

Anthony pushed his concerns away and kept moving forward. By the time he returned to the hotel, he was exhausted, jetlagged, and worn out from a long day of rehearsing. As he unbuttoned his shirt, Freddie was in his usual place by the window, looking out onto the city, his eyes scanning the sidewalks below. Now they weren't the streets of San Francisco or Barcelona, but of the sprawling metropolis of New York.

Freddie turned to him. "Anthony, I think--"

"I need to go to bed. Tomorrow is going to be a lot."

He stripped down to his boxer briefs and slipped into bed. It wasn't a lie. He needed sleep, but he'd be unlikely to get much rest with the weight of the next day on his mind. Even so, he couldn't open up another can of worms, have another conversation that would steal his focus. Freddie could wait until the performance was over to talk about his feelings.

Anthony drifted in and out of consciousness all night, fighting to keep calm. Every time he woke, Freddie was in that same position, staring out the window. Anthony knew he was unhappy, but there was nothing he could do about it.

Anthony dragged himself out of bed at nine, groggy and cranky. He wouldn't even have the crutch of coffee today. He avoided caffeine on show days — he couldn't afford to be dehydrated. Once he was in the opera house, the adrenaline would kick in and help him push through the fog of fatigue.

Anthony had a two-hour window on the actual stage of the opera house to walk through his track with Tara. The spring of the wood under his feet was energizing as his legs adjusted to the angle of the rake. He walked the path of his character, careful to be precise as possible. He wouldn't want to get hit with any moving scenery. After an hour and a half, he was confident. The opera didn't have complicated blocking, thank god. He was getting excited to show off his singing and his comedy chops.

All the while, Freddie stood to the side, silent and watching. He hadn't spoken to Anthony since the night before, instead trailing behind like a noiseless shadow. His focus had narrowed to keeping Anthony out of danger. Anthony could sense Freddie's eyes following him, snapping to any new person who came within spitting distance.

Freddie didn't speak again until the stage manager gave the call for places over the intercom in Anthony's dressing room. Gabriela and Anthony were chatting as Anthony put on his makeup, but Freddie had been standing as still as a statue against the ornate Victorian wallpaper. Anthony had been doing his best to ignore him when the announcement of 'places' came over the monitor.

"It's time, *querida*." Gabriela pulled the costume for Anthony's quick change off the rack. "We should get down there."

Anthony nodded, glancing at Freddie. For the whole day, he'd tried to put his vampire mate out of his mind, but now, at the precipice of what could be a huge moment for him, he felt a deep sadness, like the mournful tune of a cello. He'd wished for this for so many years, and he wanted this man, his boyfriend, to send him off.

Freddie must have sensed it, because he stepped forward and wrapped Anthony in his arms.

"You will be magnificent." He pressed his lips to Anthony, soft and tender. They pulsed with Freddie's care for him.

Freddie pulled back, looking deep into Anthony's eyes. "I love you, Anthony. Go and show everyone the star that you are."

Anthony's breath caught in his throat. "You love me?"

"I do." Freddie took Anthony's hand, bringing it to his mouth and kissing it. "And I believe in you."

Tears welled up, and Anthony blinked them away. He had a job to do.

"It's time." Gabriela stood by the door. Anthony nodded and left the dressing room. Freddie followed out but turned in the other direction down the hall, making his way to the front of the house.

"I'll look after him," Gabriela called to Freddie as she and Anthony headed towards the stairwell. When they reached it, she pulled open the heavy door and smiled.

"Ready?"

"Okay. Yes." Anthony stepped through and headed down the stairs, the combat boots he wore as part of his costume thumping on the concrete steps.

They were half a flight down when Gabriela put her hand on Anthony's arm, stopping his descent.

"I forgot the shoes for the change. Let me run up and fetch them. You get into places. I'll catch up with you."

Anthony nodded. He tried to focus on the show, on all the staging he had learned and all the musical phrasing. Instead he heard the sound of Freddie's voice echoing in his mind. *I love you.*

He took several more steps down when a sharp pain shot through the back of his head. As he collapsed down and his vision went blurry, he glimpsed Gabriela's face hovering over him. Poking through her cruel smirk was a pair of fangs.

Shit.

There was a faint drip drop, a trickle of water somewhere nearby, as Anthony returned consciousness. A soft murmuring tickled his ears, and then the memory of the attack came flooding back to him. He resisted the temptation to open his eyes, keeping his breath even and trying to stay still.

"Do not bother with petty deceptions, little human." The ragged rasp cut at his eardrums like a knife. "I have been a vampire for a long time. I sensed it the moment you awoke."

Anthony pondered for a second the possibility of waiting the speaker out, but he doubted it would help. Behind his back, the coarse rope rubbed raw against his wrists. He was tied to a chair.

His eyes fluttered open.

The room was dark, lit by the weak glow of an incandescent bulb peeking through a small rectangular window. The dim light revealed dirty, graffiti-covered walls and a deteriorating concrete floor. Two figures stood several feet away, shadows enveloping their bodies.

One was tall and slender, dressed in a black suit with an old-fashioned cravat. His face was hidden, but the dull warmth of the bulb illuminated his perfectly coiffed hair from behind. He was the spitting image of the stereotypical, aristocratic vampire.

The other was Gabriela.

"Glad to see I didn't do permanent damage, *querida*."

His fists balled in anger at her use of the endearment. Anthony pulled against his restraints, testing their strength. There was no give. Still, he strained against them. He had to get himself out of this.

"Gabriela is very handy with knots, little *Antonio*." It was painful for Anthony to hear the voice of the effete vamp, damaged as it was. He stepped forward, and the light revealed a strong, olive-skinned face, beautiful, except for a deep scar running across the neck that his cravat didn't fully cover. Quite beautiful, and quite familiar.

"I know you!" Anthony wracked his brain, trying to place the asshole. "Wait. You...you were in that cafe in San Francisco! When fucking Brian attacked me. You were at the next table."

"Ah yes. Brian. Not very bright, but he's dead now, so I suppose it doesn't matter. But yes, I have kept tabs on you, Anthony. Or should I say Tony, as your uncle sometimes calls you?"

"Leave my uncle out of this." Anthony strained against his restraints once more. He knew he shouldn't tire himself out, but his anger was overcoming his good sense.

The vampire smiled, self-congratulatory and malevolent. "But you're here because of your slut uncle, termite. And his bastard husband."

"Fuck you."

A stinging slashed across his face, but he hadn't seen any movement at all. Damn, the vampire was fast. Blood slid down his cheek and dripped off his chin.

"Don't goad him." Gabriela strode across the room and wiped the blood from Anthony's face with a white lace handkerchief. "Do as he says, and you'll leave alive."

"Push me, worm, and the next cut will be deeper." The vampire's eyes flashed with unhinged rage. "You'll be able to smile at your redheaded lover through your open cheek."

Anthony shuddered. The grating voice held no reason or compassion. He only hoped that Freddie would realize in time what had happened. He didn't love the idea of being the damsel in distress, but he liked the idea of dying even less.

Gabriela caught his gaze. Her face was expressionless, almost bored.

"What did I do to deserve this?" Anthony was genuinely hurt. Yes, he hadn't known her long, but he had thought they were friends.

"Nothing, darling." She patted his cheek gently where Charles had cut it. Anthony winced at the sting. "But my son is rebuilding his coven, and your new step-uncle is standing in his way."

"Your son is Charles Azarian?"

The tall vampire smirked at Anthony. "It is always lovely to be recognized."

Anthony ignored him. "You're related? To *him*? You look nothing alike."

"Child, I did not birth him." Gabriela smiled, but there was no humor there. "I sired him."

A loud rumble shook the room, growing in intensity and became overpowering, as light and shadow alternated and flickered against the wall. Dirty white flakes of old ceiling paint fell like sparse snowflakes onto Anthony's head. After a long moment, it all died down.

That was a subway train. He was sure of it. He was underground. Perhaps he wasn't that far from the opera house, but there was no way to tell.

Freddie didn't have a way to trace him here. Anthony would be used as a pawn in a vampire war he knew almost nothing about, and then he would die. And it was his fault. Freddie had supported him when his uncle and Oliver were against him coming to New York. Freddie had stood by him.

But when push came to shove, and Freddie's alarm bells were going off, Anthony hadn't trusted his boyfriend's instincts. Anthony had pushed him away, putting his career above his own safety.

Freddie was also at risk. Guilt bubbled up in his gut at the thought. If Anthony died, Freddie would follow. When he'd first heard that, it had seemed like a burden, an enormous price to pay.

Now it was Anthony's greatest concern that his own death might take down the vampire who loved him so much. The vampire who Anthony loved, even if he hadn't said the words out loud. He knew that.

Before meeting Freddie, Anthony believed in himself and only himself. His uncle, the only support system he had left, had moved to London, and Anthony had been truly and completely alone. He was his only advocate. Until Freddie.

Freddie wanted him to have all the success he wished for. He stood up for Anthony, and when it came down to it, Anthony had ignored his feelings. But Freddie hadn't run. He'd been unhappy, angry even. But he'd continued to love Anthony and stand by him.

He was Anthony's mate, a word that had meanings Anthony was only now learning. He'd proved himself worthy of Anthony's trust and his love.

Closing his eyes, he sent a thought towards Freddie. Perhaps there was some kind of mate magic he wasn't aware of that would allow him to communicate, that would let Freddie hear him.

I'm underground, in a room. There was a train. I'm not sure if I'm at a station or not.

He waited for a response, but there was nothing. Maybe a slight twinge in his chest, but that was probably anxiety. He opened his eyes.

"What happens now?" His voice shook as he asked the question. He hated how weak he sounded.

"Now, little lanternfly, we wait for Oliver Hughes to respond to our summons." Charles winked at him. "Then we negotiate."

Anthony wriggled again, stretching the knots of the restraints.

"Freddie will come for me."

"We are not novices, maggot-food. The Azarian coven has had control of the abandoned stations in Manhattan for almost a decade now. No one will find you."

We're in an abandoned subway station. Please come for me, Freddie. I...I love you.

21

FREDDIE

As Freddie sat in the front row of the opera house, staring at the lush velvet curtain, his emotions churned in his gut. He was proud, so proud of Anthony, that he would make his debut at Manhattan Lyric Opera. He was thrilled and nervous to watch his love perform, but it wasn't enough to overcome the dread that the Azarians might take advantage of their few minutes apart to attack.

As the orchestra took up the strains of the overture, the mournful sound of the French horn washed over Freddie.

The opera began, and Freddie found it hard to focus on the chorus of villagers, or even on the lively soprano who played the title character of *La fille du régiment*. She was doing well, as far as Freddie could tell. She was certainly loud. But he was itching to see the face of his beloved.

As the chorus of soldiers filed in, Freddie's whole body tensed. He knew that something was amiss. He'd watched Anthony rehearse the entire show, running staging and traffic patterns in their hotel room. He knew the soldiers should be chasing Anthony, but his mate wasn't on stage.

With a confused look on his face, the baritone sang the line that would require Anthony's vocal response.

"Eh quoi! c'est l'étranger qui t'aime!..."

The silence that followed lasted an eternity. Before the stage manager could get on the microphone to stop the show, Freddie was out of his seat and had leapt onto the stage, not caring in the slightest that the audience of humans might question his supernatural athleticism.

"Come!" he cried out as he hit the stage, and Rose and Lillian dove from their two parterre boxes on either side of the proscenium.. Lillian fell into a roll, and Rose caught herself with her hands as she hit the deck.

They trailed behind Freddie as he rushed backstage, weaving in and out amongst the confused stagehands and supernumeraries. He couldn't scent his lover anywhere.

"He never even made it backstage!" he yelled as Rose and Lillian caught up with him.

"The stairwell from the dressing room is back there." Rose gestured to an exit off in the stage left wing.

Metal screamed as Freddie ripped the door from its hinges, bounding up the concrete steps three at a time. The scent of his mate's blood stopped him in his tracks.

"He's been hurt." The growl ripped from his throat, and his vision clouded over with the red mist. He was losing control.

The slap across his face came hard and stinging. "You can't rage right now." Lillian brushed the hair from her face nonchalantly. "We need you here with us. Find Anthony."

He squeezed his eyes tight. Freddie fought back against the crimson surge that threatened to overwhelm him. Locked in place, he was striving to keep his wits about him. Two firm hands pressed against his cheeks, and Rose's voice cut through the fog.

"Your demon can trust us, Freddie. We will find him. You are not alone."

His eyes popped open, and his breath burst from his lungs as he struggled for control of himself.

"My mate…I have to…"

"I know," Rose said. "We're here. I've fought under you. You've protected the coven with courage, even while you held yourself apart from us. Now you've found your mate. That is not a weakness. It is not a weakness to connect. We're here. We won't let you down."

Rose's eyes sparkled with determined compassion, and the wild rage flared inside him and died down. It wasn't gone, but it was under his control.

He nodded. "Thank you."

Rose removed her hands and stepped back. Freddie knelt down where the odor of Anthony's blood was the strongest. There were traces of it on the steps, but nothing to indicate a fatal blow.

"He is alive. Unconscious, I think. His dresser, Gabriela, was here, but I can't smell anyone else."

"How well do you know her?" Rose's eyes turned sharp and cold.

"Well enough. Anthony worked with her in Barcelona and he asked her to come along. She was charming and did her job well."

"She became his personal dresser after only a couple of weeks?"

Freddie nodded, then blinked, confused. It was odd that he hadn't even questioned it.

"Was she charming, or did she Charm you?" Lillian chimed in uneasily. "In the way of the old world vampires?"

"It's...it's possible. She'd have to be older than me, though, much older, old enough that she could Charm me without my knowledge. There are only a handful of vampires left who are that ancient, and I know all of them. I've never seen her before."

As he finished his words, he let out a gasp and touched his cheek. No blood, but that was the sting of a claw or knife cut. He was sure of it. Rage rumbled in his chest.

"Whoever has him is going to die," Freddie growled.

"What was that?" Lillian asked.

"Anthony is my mate. I think...I'm feeling his pain through the bond, even though we haven't completed it. We need to figure out who did this, and where they've taken him."

Rose and Lillian made eye contact, dread on their faces.

"What's wrong?"

"Gabriela de Aragon." Rose took a deep breath. "She died decades before you joined the coven. A mutually fatal fight with a thousand-year-old vamp from the Carpathian Mountains."

"Or at least we *thought* she died." Lillian sighed in frustration. "She had a tendency to turn sociopathic humans into vampires."

"She sired Charles Azarian," Rose said, her eyes hard.

Freddie growled and punched the wall of the stairwell. The surface of the concrete crumbled at the blow, and cracks spidered down to the floor. He surveyed the area one more time and sniffed.

"Whether it was Gabriela or Azarian or someone else, they cleaned up well. There's no scent trail from here. We have no way of following."

"The Azarians have multiple strongholds in Manhattan," Lillian said. "They have several large ships docked on the Hudson somewhere around 55th, and they've got their claws in the Metropolitan Museum of Art and hideouts underneath—"

I'm underground, in a room. There was a train. I'm not sure if I'm at a station or not.

Freddie put his hand up, cutting Lillian off as Anthony's voice filled his mind. "He's underground." He closed his eyes, trying to concentrate.

That Anthony could communicate while still human spoke to the strength of their bond, and the intensity of his emotions. The sending was faint, but it was there.

I'm coming, my love. Freddie doubted the words would reach him, considering Anthony was human, but even if the specifics didn't come through, the intention might. Freddie opened his eyes.

"Wherever he is, he can hear the train."

"The Azarians have control of several tunnels," Lillian said. "It has to be somewhere near here."

We're in an abandoned subway station. Please come for me, Freddie...

"They're in an abandoned station." Freddie shouted. "We have to get to him!"

"91st Street Station." Lillian started bounding down the stairs, and Freddie followed. "That's the closest of their hideouts."

"I'll catch up." Rose had her phone out. "Garrett needs to know where we're going."

They moved with inhuman speed, darting between pedestrians and cars so quickly that Freddie doubted anyone even sensed they were there. Fear pulsed through his bond from Anthony. It spurred him on.

When they reached the doors, Freddie snapped the padlock off like a toothpick, and kicked the thick metal door, which collapsed in half. They were down the stairs in a moment, and the minute they hit the platform level, Freddie could hear Anthony's heartbeat, fast but still strong.

The sound pulled Freddie forward. He followed it towards an area of the station that must have been closed to the public. As he almost reached it, a voice in his mind stopped him in his tracks.

Freddie. Report, Master Hughes commanded.

They have Anthony. I'm going to kill Charles Azarian.

Waves of disapproval pulsed through the coven master's bond with him.

No. Give us time to get there.

Freddie froze, paralyzed. He could not disobey Master Hughes, but his mate was in danger, steps away.

Master...

No, Freddie. We have to—

Freddie sensed the whimper through the incomplete mate bond before it hit his ears. Anthony was hurt. Taking a few steps closer, the rusty aroma of his love's fresh blood hit his nose.

He's injured. The old law releases me from your command.

Freddie!

There were few things that modern vampire society held onto from the bad old days, when the only rule was "might makes right." The one sacrosanct tenet from the beginning was that the safety of one's mate overrode any other command. Partly because the death of the vampire's mate would be followed swiftly by their own, and partly because the pain at a mate's injury was incapacitating.

Freddie burst into the room, flinging the door off to one side. Inside the dirty, deteriorating subway office, a tall, effete vampire flinched, fear flashing on his perfect face. That had to be Charles Azarian.

Gabriela showed no emotion. Her clawed hand was around Anthony's throat.

The crimson surge no longer fought to control Freddie. His demon knew Freddie would give it the blood and carnage it desired.

"Gabriela de Aragon."

"Ah, the muscle finally did some research." Gabriela's voice wasn't angry or maniacal. It was matter of fact, as if the situation was a mundane business transaction.

Freddie sensed Lillian enter behind him and stand off his right shoulder. "Why aren't you dead?" she asked.

"Some decrepit Carpathian hermit couldn't take me out. But he was a convenient excuse. Too many people were interested in my comings and goings. I needed a new beginning."

"Don't talk to them, Mother!" The words poured out of Charles Azarian in a hoarse screech. "Until we can set up a meeting with Oliver, we have nothing to say."

Freddie turned to the tall vampire, whose petulant expression betrayed his calm elegance. "I speak for my master."

"Bullshit! I want to see Oliver."

Rose entered and flanked Freddie on the left. "The coven master is mated, married, and has an empire to run. He has no time for your petty desires." Her bitter tone echoed her twin's.

"Oliver is mine! His coven is mine!" Charles touched the scar on his throat as if reliving a memory. "When Oliver betrayed me, when he gave me *this*, he forfeited his life. All of you will serve me."

"I don't think so." Freddie took a step towards him.

"Mother!" Charles let out a shrill whine as he stomped his foot like a child.

Anthony yelped as Gabriela's claw tightened around his throat.

"No, no, no. None of that," she said.

The powerful grip pressed around Freddie's own throat as he experienced Anthony's pain secondhand. Freddie's veins burned with their need to punish his mate's attacker. Rose placed a hand on his arm to steady him.

"Yes, calm the brute." Charles was still vibrating with anxious energy, but his smirk showed that he thought he had the upper hand. "Dear Freddie wouldn't want to see his mate's lifeblood spill out on the dirty concrete."

A sharp growl sounded from the door. As one, they turned to see the source. Garrett stood in the doorway, his eyes feral and his claws long and sharp, more animal than human.

The room erupted into chaos.

Garrett flew across the floor in a storm of bloodlust, separating Gabriela from Anthony and slamming her into the nearby wall. Rose and Lillian lunged for Charles, and Freddie was at Anthony's side in an instant, his claws slicing through the ropes that bound Anthony's hands.

"My mate..." Freddie's words caught in his throat.

"I called to you. You heard me." Anthony rubbed the wrists of his now-freed hands. He brought them up to rest on Freddie's chest.

Freddie nodded, getting lost in Anthony's eyes as he looked down at him. "You are mine. I will always come for you."

"I love you." Anthony's eyes shone in the dim light. "I do."

Freddie kissed him, hard and desperate, needing to feel his mate, to calm the demon beast inside of him. He would never allow himself to be separated from Anthony. Anthony would never face this kind of danger again.

A loud shriek broke through their quiet bubble, and Freddie slid in front of Anthony. No one would get near his mate.

22

ANTHONY

Gabriela and Garrett clawed ferociously at each other. Garrett was a beast, a creature of naked fury, but Gabriela was giving as good as she got, a look of prime disinterest on her face. Her blasé ferocity made Anthony squirm. Was she bored by all this?

"She's very old, and very, very strong." Freddie had sensed his confusion. "Not much can touch her. Stay out of her line of sight."

In the far corner of the room, Lillian and Rose had flanked Charles, who stood flat against the wall like a cornered cobra, reared and waiting to strike.

Freddie lifted Anthony's chair by the leg and smashed it. Left with a jagged piece of wood in his hand, he picked away at the end with inhuman speed, extending his claws and sharpening it to a point. He handed the newly made stake to Anthony.

"If worst comes to worst, use this. Aim for the heart."

"Freddie..."

A sharp cry came from Rose. Three claw marks ran across her face. They were weeping blood. She had gotten too close to Charles. Although she was in pain, she quickly recovered, growling at her attacker and shifting to keep him in his place.

"They need my help," Freddie whispered into Anthony's ear. "Don't underestimate Charles and Gabriela. Don't draw attention to yourself. Stay back, and only use the stake in self-defense."

Anthony nodded, not trusting himself to say anything. Freddie hugged Anthony hard, then turned to enter the fray.

Garrett was terrifying, a whirlwind of fangs and claws, but Gabriela was flowing around him, wielding a long, thin steel stiletto. She gave as good as she got, the wounds she inflicted biting deep into Garrett's flesh. Anthony wondered that she didn't use her own claws in fighting, but she was an expert in her weapon. Evenly matched, they were a blur of motion to Anthony's human sight.

Charles was still, his eyes glaring out in petty defiance from atop his cravat. The defensive position suited him. He lashed out when either Rose or Lillian got close, but otherwise stood like a statue, peering out at his enemies.

As Freddie reached them, Rose and Lillian made eye contact and attacked together. In one quick movement, faster than would seem possible, Charles grabbed each by the throat and hurled them against the opposite walls. Anthony heard the crunching of bones as the twin vampires hit, sliding to the floor. Both were still moving, but they were hurting.

Anthony backed away from the action, staying equidistant from the two fights. He grasped the sharpened chair leg tight in his hands. His instincts screamed he would never survive a fight with any of them, but his heart raced. He wished desperately to help Freddie. His eyes darted back and forth, keeping track of all the fighting.

He would never forgive himself if Freddie died rescuing him.

Freddie did not allow Charles to keep him at a distance, barreling in and grappling him, but the Azarian coven master was deceptively strong for someone with his slender frame. They locked together, straining with effort. Freddie growled like a jungle cat. Charles' eyes betrayed a flash of fear, but in a second it was gone, hidden behind his arrogant mask.

Gabriela and Garrett continued to give one for one. Both of them were tiring, their movements growing slower. As she whirled around, evading one of Garrett's claw strikes, she caught Anthony's gaze and raised her eyebrow.

"It didn't have to be like this, *querida*. Now all of you have to die."

The statement cost her, as her split concentration allowed Garrett to slash deep into her side. She flinched. It was the first time she'd shown any emotion during the fight.

Anthony berated himself. Freddie had told Anthony to avoid being noticed by her. His back to the wall, he inched away from her and Garrett, but could only go so far without getting pulled into the other brawl.

Freddie forced Charles out a few feet, and they strained against each other, their arms locked together. They both bled where their fingertips touched skin. Their claws had dug into the other's flesh.

Anthony flinched at the brutality of the fight. Freddie had dragged Charles from his defensive position, but he wasn't doing well. Charles hissed and lunged, trying to tear out Freddie's throat with his fangs. Freddie kept him at bay, but barely. Given time, Charles would overcome him. Azarian was fueled by some kind of perverted need for blood that Freddie couldn't match.

Then the moment came. The two vampires rotated as they struggled with each other. Charles' back was bare to Anthony. He lunged once again for Freddie, grazing his throat. Anthony saw a trickle of blood run down Freddie's long neck.

A red mist appeared in front of his eyes, and suddenly it was as if the spirit of some ancient beast had inhabited Anthony. He was in motion before he could stop himself. With a strength he'd never known, he plunged the wooden stake into Charles Azarian's back.

The squeal was painful, so loud that Anthony collapsed down to his knees, clutching his ears. The scream cowed whatever power had taken Anthony over. As it died down, he looked up to see Charles seizing on the ground, blood flowing from his wound.

Anthony locked eyes with Freddie, smiling. Although he was bent over, and bleeding from dozens of lacerations, Freddie smiled back.

The smile turned into a scream of fear, as something pierced Anthony's torso. There was a horrible burning in his gut, like someone had impaled him on a hot poker. He looked down to see Gabriela's stiletto knife buried in his stomach.

The last thing he saw as everything faded was Freddie flying across the room, claws outstretched, desperate to end Gabriela's life.

The last thing he heard was Freddie's anguished scream.

Then there was nothing.

For a long time, there was nothing.

The overwhelming smell of iron, but no light, no sound. Just darkness. He couldn't even feel himself breathe. Was he breathing?

It may have been eternity, or it may have been seconds. Anthony didn't know. His consciousness drifted until pain forced him back, a terrible blaze spreading throughout his entire body.

He had a body. It hurt, it hurt worse than anything he'd ever experienced, but it was there.

He tried to breathe.

Razor blades invaded his throat, the air itself an icy poison. He whimpered, scared that any movement would increase the torture, but he forced his eyes open.

The light must have been dim, just a flickering candle, but it was so bright it was as if his retinas had blown out. His vision was overexposed and blurry. He squinted, groaning.

"You are okay, my love. I am here."

Anthony couldn't move his head to look. He gave his pupils a moment to adjust to the room. When he spoke, his voice was a weak whisper.

"Freddie?"

The face of Anthony's mate came into focus. The terrified concern there hurt Anthony's heart.

Despite the pain, Anthony was overjoyed that Freddie was alive.

"Take it slow, my sweet," Freddie said. "You've been through a lot."

"What happened?"

Freddie's brow furrowed. "Don't worry about—"

"Please, Freddie." Anthony lifted his hand to Freddie's forearm, squeezing with what little energy he had. "I need to know. What happened?"

Freddie sighed, and with his free arm reached to a small, mahogany nightstand. Anthony's eyes had adjusted such that he could see the entire room now. It was an elegant but simply furnished white bedroom. He lay in a four-poster bed. A bit of greenery was visible through the window next to him.

"Drink some water, and I'll tell you."

Freddie lifted the old-fashioned crystal glass to his lips, and Anthony let the liquid spill into his mouth. It hurt going down, but as it did, a cool feeling spread, soothing his ragged throat. When it hit his stomach, though, there was a wave of nausea, but it subsided quickly enough.

"What do you remember?"

Anthony blinked. "I...I staked him. Azarian. The bastard."

Freddie stroked his forehead, and the ache in his bones calmed a little.

"You did, my love. I'm so proud of you. If you hadn't, I don't know how that fight would have ended."

"He's dead?" Sudden dread filled him. He couldn't keep running from the asshole. "He has to be, right?"

"You hit his heart. His death was inevitable. Do you remember what happened next?"

"I...Gabriela!" Anthony's hand went to his stomach, searching for the wound, but all he found was the faintest of scars. "She gutted me. But...I shouldn't have healed so fast."

"No, you shouldn't have." A nervous look came over Freddie's face. He was tiptoeing around something. "Gabriela was more powerful than we imagined. Garrett is formidable, but she had the upper hand. When you took out her son, she threw Garrett off and attacked you."

"Did you kill her?"

"No. She was fast. Faster than me, even. She escaped down the subway tunnels."

"Oh." Anthony ran his fingers along his stomach. "But how am I okay? How long has it been? Where are we?"

"We're in London, in the coven house in Knightsbridge. It was the safest place. The fight was three days ago."

"Three days! Shouldn't I be in a hospital?"

Freddie gazed deep into Anthony's eyes, and Anthony's breath caught. Freddie was so vulnerable, and Anthony hated what he saw in his face. Fear.

"You'd be in hospital if you were still human. But you're not."

"What?"

"Gabriela was vicious. You lost so much blood. You would have died." Freddie paused, as if finding the courage to continue. "I had to turn you."

Anthony stared at his mate, trying to process his words. He was a vampire now? He didn't feel any different. He was still himself, although a version of himself who'd been run over by an eighteen-wheeler.

Freddie shifted back and forth, as if the silence was making him uncomfortable. He spoke with a nervous desperation.

"I'm so sorry, Anthony. We never discussed it. I wasn't sure if you wanted to be turned, but I had to save you. I couldn't lose you, not when I'd finally found you—"

Anthony lifted himself up and kissed Freddie, ignoring the pain. It was clumsy, their positions awkward, but it didn't matter. Anthony put all of his feelings for Freddie into that kiss: his gratitude, his admiration, and his love.

Freddie wrapped his arms around Anthony's back and guided him down to the mattress again. He pulled away.

"Anthony—"

"Freddie, you saved my life. Why would you ever think I wouldn't want this? I get to stay by your side for hundreds of years. It's the greatest gift."

"Yes, but you'll have to drink blood…"

"I don't have to kill humans, do I?"

"Vampires haven't done that in over a century. And if they do, we stop them."

"Then I'll be fine. More than fine. I'll have an incredible life. A life with you."

A tear trailed down Freddie's cheek. Had he been so terrified that Anthony would reject him? Anthony vowed Freddie would never have to feel that way again.

Freddie kissed him on the forehead. Anthony yawned, unable to help himself.

"Rest, my sweet. Your body is recovering from the transformation. I had to drain your blood and replace it with mine. Your abilities are still developing."

Anthony nodded and closed his eyes. A gentle lub-dub reached his ears. Was that...was that Freddie's heartbeat? The beginning of his enhanced supernatural senses?

The sweet, steady beat of his mate's heart lulled him to perfect sleep.

23

FREDDIE

"**T**he danger has passed. There's no need to watch him sleep."

Freddie looked up at his master from his chair at Anthony's bedside, not releasing his grip on Anthony's hand. Master Hughes waited in the doorway, dressed to the nines in a tan three-piece suit. His face was lined with exhaustion. This couldn't have been easy on him, either.

"I've always watched him," Freddie said. "That is my job. I won't stop now."

Master Hughes sighed. Freddie wasn't sure where he stood with the coven-master. Anthony was safe, but in the process he'd been made a vampire. Charles Azarian was dead, in theory, a good thing, but Freddie didn't know if the master harbored any guilt about his former lover. And Gabriela de Aragon was out there somewhere. Eventually, she'd have to be dealt with.

Most of all, Freddie had disobeyed Master Hughes' command. He had a right to, according to the old law. But that just meant the coven master wouldn't kill him in retribution. He still might demote him, or toss him out of the coven altogether.

Despite that, Freddie couldn't bear to release Anthony's hand and stand, even if it would be a sign of respect for Master Hughes. He wouldn't let go of his sleeping mate. He'd come so close to losing him.

"Very well." Master Hughes approached the bed, sitting down opposite Freddie, his muscular frame dwarfing the small wooden chair that his mate had been using during his own vigil with Anthony. Daniel had been by Anthony's side for the first couple of days, but once Anthony had come through the change unscathed, he'd let him rest alone.

Freddie's demon would not allow him to leave his mate by himself. He'd come too close to losing him.

"Where do you expect to live?" Master Hughes asked.

Freddie tensed. He had hoped that the coven master would give them some time.

"I...I don't know. I hadn't thought that far ahead. Anthony travels, so it doesn't matter too much. I'll have to talk to him."

"You disobeyed my direct order and put my husband's nephew in danger." Master Hughes' tone was sharp, his gaze piercing.

"I don't regret it."

"No." A small, sad smile appeared on Master Hughes' face, and the man's whole body relaxed. Freddie had never seen him look so unguarded. "I won't hold it against you. I know what it is to have your mate under threat."

"Oh." The coven master wasn't throwing them out? "What does it matter where we live?"

"Because I have a proposition for you, Freddie, although my mate will probably be quite angry with me. He has dreams of Anthony living here with us. But Charles Azarian is dead, and the once-enormous coven of New York is now a handful of young, directionless vamps. They need a coven master."

Freddie stared at the man who'd saved him, who'd given him a home and a purpose when he was desperate for one. He couldn't be asking what Freddie thought he was asking.

"I thought you wanted me to be your First..."

"That was my plan. But I need someone in New York, someone I can trust, with a strong enough hand to bring the wild ones to heel or dispose of them. Someone who can also be diplomatic if the situation requires."

"Me?" Freddie shook his head. "I'm no good at diplomacy."

"You've changed, Freddie." Freddie could hear the pride in his master's voice, and it warmed him. "You are more open now. Anthony will be the perfect coven master's mate. When you get too grumpy, he can help smooth things over."

"Grumpy?!" Freddie grimaced.

"Yes, my friend. You can be a grumpy old man. Anthony will help keep you from committing too many faux pas."

Freddie looked down at Anthony's face, snoring, angelic in repose. "I'll have to speak to my mate. I don't know if he'll want to be a coven master's mate. He may not want to live in New York."

"Of course."

"What of Gabriela?" Freddie asked. His demon was uneasy that the one who had hurt his mate was still out there, rather than dead by his hands.

Master Hughes stood. "She's left the US. Beyond that, I can't say. We can't trust that she'll leave us alone."

"No."

Master Hughes walked around the bed, squeezing Freddie's shoulder. His hand was strong. It was a strength Freddie had depended upon over the years.

"Anthony will be awake soon. His transformation is complete. You have much to discuss."

Freddie nodded. "Thank you, master."

"I'm no longer your master, Freddie. We can be equals. And friends." A wide smile appeared on his face. "Call me Oliver."

Freddie's mind reeled. He'd served under Master Hughes for decades. Being his friend would be quite the change.

"Thank you...Oliver." The name sounded like an alien language in Freddie's mouth. "For everything."

His coven master, or perhaps now his ex-coven master, patted his back and departed. Freddie sat there, studying Anthony's face, watching his chest rise and fall. He'd never imagined he'd have a mate, never mind one so beautiful. He would go anywhere, do anything for this man.

Freddie closed his eyes and took a breath, squeezing Anthony's hand. It was a tempting offer, to have his own coven. The thought of so many depending on him stirred up a deep fear in Freddie's chest, but maybe that was a good sign. He had a responsibility to those left without a master after the death of Charles Azarian. They were young, and they'd been turned by a sociopath. It was a fate he understood well.

They deserved better.

"You're thinking so hard…"

Freddie looked down to see Anthony's sweet smile, his bright eyes gazing up at him.

"You're awake." Freddie stroked Anthony's cheek with the back of his hand. "How do you feel?"

"Good." Anthony stretches his arms over his head, yawning. "Better than good, I could run a marathon."

"You could, and beat every human alive."

"I need to sit up." Freddie reached out to help, but Anthony was up, scooching his back against the headboard with ease. "It's as if I was never ill."

"The transformation is complete."

Anthony gave Freddie a heated look. "Oh, really?" A pair of fangs dropped from his upper lip, the enamel gleaming.

A deep warmth spread throughout Freddie's chest. He was relieved. He was turned on. Hell, he was happy. It was an unfamiliar sensation.

Before he could respond, Anthony was on him, kissing and nibbling, letting the tips of his fangs snag on Freddie's lips. It sent electric shocks down his spine. A single drop of blood leaked from his pierced skin.

Anthony licked it up with his tongue. Freddie watched as Anthony's pupils flashed red, and a low growl escaped from his throat.

"Holy fuck." Anthony squeezed his eyes shut in a look of ecstasy. "What is this?"

"I am your sire, and you are my mate. Your blood is my blood, and blood calls to blood. You can drink human blood, but you can also drink from me. Drinking from your mate invigorates the body and soul."

"You can drink from me?" Anthony shivered, and ran his hand down Freddie's neck. In an instant, his fingernails stretched out into claws, and he sliced Freddie's black t-shirt open.

"I can. You drank from me when you were dying, even though you don't remember it. Now that you are fully turned, when I drink from you, it will complete our mating."

Freddie grabbed Anthony by the chin with some force. He no longer had to worry about Anthony's human frailty. He kissed Anthony hard. Anthony ran his claws down Freddie's side.

"And that was my favorite t-shirt."

"A plain black tee was your favorite?" Anthony laughed as he slipped a clawed finger into the waistband of Freddie's pants. "I don't like you with clothes on."

Freddie grabbed Anthony by the wrist. Anthony struggled against him, a playful, fiery lust in his eyes.

"Soon, my love. We have something to talk about."

Anthony relaxed backwards against the bed, resigned. "What the hell else could there be?"

"I wish you would rest a while longer—"

"I'm awake, Freddie. If I rest anymore, I'll tear down the curtains in boredom."

"Fine." Freddie interlaced his fingers with Anthony's. He loved how much bigger his hand was than his mate's. "Master Hughes wishes me to become the coven master in Manhattan."

"Really?"

"Yes. But I'll not be parted from you. If you don't wish to live there, we won't go. We can stay here in London. We could go anywhere."

"I would love to be in New York." Anthony paused, and Freddie sensed a twinge of sadness. "Although I can't imagine the Manhattan Lyric would want me back after I disappeared on opening night."

Freddie leaned back in his chair, unable to stop the shit-eating grin that appeared on his face. "I took care of that for you."

"What does that mean?" Anthony squinted, suspicious.

"I made it clear that you were abducted because of Mr. Fitzpatrick's negligence in keeping me from backstage. He was desperate to avoid a scandal, and it wasn't hard to get him to schedule you next season. Give him a call. He'll be very accommodating. He'll let you name the opera and the role."

"How...why would he agree to all that?"

"Strange thing." Freddie chuckled, running his fingers through Anthony's hair. "Seems that merry old General Manager Henry Fitzpatrick knows about vampires. He had dealings with the Azarian coven. Some less-than-legal real estate transactions. Some of my men found evidence at the New York covenhouse. Once I threatened to go to the authorities, he was extremely excited to help."

"You blackmailed the general manager of the most important opera house in the world?" Anthony's brows furrowed.

Freddie nodded, hoping he hadn't overstepped. "Happy new birthday?"

"That's incredible. *You're* incredible."

"So…"

"So I guess we're moving to New York." Anthony reached over and ran his hand down Freddie's chest, grazing his right nipple. At his touch, electricity sparked on Freddie's skin. "And we're going to run a coven?"

"Seems that way."

Anthony thought for a moment, then his eyes lit up. "I'm going to throw fabulous parties."

"I can't wait." Freddie attempted to keep the sarcasm out of his response, although he wasn't sure he succeeded.

With a growl, Anthony flipped Freddie out of his chair and onto the bed, straddling him. Freddie laughed out loud. Anthony was discovering his vampire strength and speed. This was going to be fun. Anthony pinned Freddie's hands behind his head, bending down to whisper in his ear.

"I need you. We can do slow and tender later."

Freddie struggled against Anthony's grasp. He was applying actual force now. He ground his ass against Freddie's now-hard cock and moaned, soft and low.

"I'm going to ride you, and then you are going to bite me."

"Whatever you need, my love."

Anthony let go of Freddie's hands and sliced off his own underwear in one motion. His cock sprang free, bouncing on Freddie's stomach, dribbling pre-cum onto his hard, pale abs. Anthony unbuttoned Freddie's dress pants. Freddie shuddered as Anthony's hand found his dick, squeezing along its length and pulling it out through the zipper.

"There's lube—"

Anthony slammed down onto him, and Freddie was enveloped in Anthony's tight warmth. Anthony let out a ragged groan.

"I need to feel it," he said with a gleam in his eye. "I'll heal fast, right?"

"In seconds, love."

Anthony rocked gently back and forth, his hands clutching the sides of Freddie's rib cage. The tingle of Freddie's orgasm was gathering in his balls. This first round would not last long.

Anthony smiled. "It already doesn't hurt." With that, Anthony set a devastating pace, bouncing on Freddie's dick. Freddie loved the smack of Anthony's beautiful ass slapping against the muscle of his thighs. Anthony was almost screaming with need. "Please, more, I need it."

"I'm so close..." Freddie's voice was ragged.

"Yes, I need you to fill me up."

If possible, Anthony moved faster and harder. He was squeezing Freddie's cock with his ass, trying to milk the cum out of him.

As Freddie approached the point of no return, he wrapped his hands around Anthony's waist, tucked his feet under him and *pushed*, using his vampiric strength to propel them across the room.

Anthony hit the wall with Freddie still inside of him, and Freddie folded him in half, pushing his legs back against his shoulders as he fucked him into the drywall.

"Fucking god!" Anthony's eyes squeezed shut. "You're so deep, yes, please."

Freddie was in control now, and he was relentless in pursuit of his orgasm. Eventually, he would spend hours inside Anthony, days even. He would fuck him again with his own cum as lube. Just the thought brought him to the edge.

"Do you want it, my love?"

"Yes. Please. I need you to…"

Freddie took in the gorgeous man in front of him, the thick muscles of his thighs straining, his eyes desperate. Freddie pushed deeper into Anthony. The sounds he made were glorious.

"Are you sure?"

"Yes. Now, Freddie, I need it!"

A growl ripped from Freddie's throat as he exploded inside of Anthony. His orgasm seemed never ending, filling his lover's perfect ass. Anthony screamed and shook against him.

When he slowed, Anthony looked up at him, sated, but with mischief in his eyes.

"What?" Freddie knew Anthony couldn't be trusted.

Anthony's fangs dropped, and he lunged for Freddie's neck, piercing the skin and drinking deeply.

Freddie was instantly hard and once again on the precipice of orgasm. Freddie slammed into Anthony, harder and harder, unable to resist the temptation. Anthony screamed as Freddie bit down on his own neck, even as Freddie emptied himself once more into his mate. It was so intense, so overwhelming. It was perfect.

Then their mate bond snapped into place, and they were as one. There was no separation between them now. Their emotions, their desires, all were an open book. The love pulsed between them like an electric current.

As the second orgasm subsided, Freddie's legs wobbled with exhaustion. He folded his arms around Anthony, his mate's own release rubbing off on his stomach as they made contact and guided him down as they slid from the wall to the floor. He stayed inside Anthony, savoring the connection with the man he loved.

Anthony wrapped tight around him, licking at the puncture wound on Freddie's neck. Freddie did the same, but with tiny flicks of his tongue that he knew would send electricity sparking across Anthony's skin. Freddie loved to feel him tremble in his arms.

"You are more than I deserve in a mate." Freddie whispered into Anthony's ear. "I will love you always. I wear your mark to prove it, and you wear mine."

"I love you..." Anthony was barely conscious, worn out from the first real expenditure of energy after his turning. A moment later, he was snoring into Freddie's shoulder.

Without jostling him, Freddie moved them both off the floor and to the bed.

He would spend the rest of eternity caring for this man, and he wouldn't regret a second of it. He was certain of it.

Epilogue
Six Months Later

ANTHONY

Anthony took a deep breath as he watched **the opera from the wings,** waiting for his entrance. Enzo, the hilarious bass playing Don Magnifico in this production of *La Cenerentola*, was hamming it up big time, waltzing around the set in bright red bloomers, taunting the two singers who were portraying his daughters. The audience was eating it up.

Across the expanse of the set, in the stage right wings, a woman in a flowered corset and a simple white skirt smiled and waved at him. It was Lena. Anthony had made sure she was playing the lead for this production. She'd been a good friend to him, and she deserved all the success in the world. Of course she was his Cinderella.

Anthony was making his Manhattan Lyric debut. This milestone, something that he hadn't thought would happen for a decade, if ever, was waiting steps in front of him. He was a few bars of music away from singing the first notes.

In some ways, it wasn't as big of a deal now. So much had changed. He no longer had the desperation of the ticking clock on his career. He didn't have to kill himself to make his debut at every major opera house. He had time.

He also had perspective. He could enjoy this profession, but eventually people would notice that he wasn't aging. When that happened, he would need to do something else, to become someone else. As he looked at the long years stretching out ahead, the details of his job no longer seemed all that important.

He could just savor this moment, the music, and his mate beside him.

He smiled at Freddie, who stood in the darkness to Anthony's right. There was no real reason for him to be backstage. They were in charge of the New York coven now, and no one was trying to kidnap or kill him. They hadn't seen hide nor hair of Gabriela de Aragon.

But it felt like a corrective to have Freddie here, watching from the wings.

Freddie smiled back, his face beaming with pride, his fangs flashing white in the backstage shadows.

The coven was a work in progress, and there'd been some growing pains, certainly. But one thing had remained steady: Freddie's support and love for him. Everything they'd accomplished, they'd done together.

Like they were together right now.

"Are you ready for your debut, Antonio Bianchi?" Freddie smiled, and Anthony's heart sang. Those smiles would always only be for him.

"Not Antonio." Anthony leaned into him. "Not anymore. I'm happy to just be Anthony. That's enough."

Freddie's arms wrapped around him, and he could feel so much through their bond: respect, admiration, devotion.

"Break a leg, my love." Freddie's whisper brushed against his ear.

Out there, the house was filled with opening night patrons, critics, and friends. Uncle Daniel and Oliver sat front row center, waiting to see him make his entrance. But right here, with Freddie, everything was perfect.

The music swelled, and the magic of the stage called to Anthony. He had so much magic now. "It's time."

Squeezing Freddie's hand once, Anthony let go, stepped out, and began to sing.

J.B. Warrick is a writer of MM paranormal and supernatural romance. They live in New York City, and when they're not writing they spend their time eating delicious snacks and listening to opera. If you're looking for fast-moving open-door romance, fun and magic, and just a touch of darkness, J.B.'s books are for you!

The next book in the Vampire Impresario series, *The Baritone's Rival*, will be released in January of 2025.

J.B. Warrick also writes MM fantasy romance under the name K.L. Larsen. Check out their arranged-marriaged, enemies-to-lovers fantasy romance *The Last of the Dark Lords*.

www.jbwarrick.com

Acknowledgments

J.B. would like to thank Allen for his inspiration and his incredible feedback. Without him this book would never have been finished. Thanks as well to the folks of the Bookdun Challenge Discord server.